Meet Inspector Safiotte.

My big signet ring cut his cheek open, and I felt the bone in his nose give as my fist caught it on the side. . . .

The blood flowed and was absorbed in a widening blot by the green blotting-pad on the desk. . . .

I went into the toilet, took a towel, and soaked it in cold water, and came back. I hit him a few smacks on the back of the head. . . .

"You can hear me?" I said.

It took a big effort, but he nodded.

"Who?" I said.

Meet Staccato Crime.

The rhythm of classic noir.

BODIES ARE DUST
by
P. J. Wolfson

Introduction
by
David Rachels

An Imprint of Stark House Press

Published by Staccato Crime
An imprint of Stark House Press
1315 H Street
Eureka, CA 95501, USA
griffinskye3@sbcglobal.net
www.starkhousepress.com

ISBN: 978-1-95147347-1
Staccato Crime: SC-001

All Staccato Crime titles are edited and produced
by David Rachels and Jeff Vorzimmer.
Book series design by ¡caliente!design, Austin, Texas

First Staccato Crime Edition: June 2021

Acknowledgments

The staff at Staccato Crime would like to thank the following people for their various contributions to the project of bringing *Bodies Are Dust* back into print after 60 long years: Allan Guthrie, who tirelessly promoted this title toward that end; and also, Jeff Pickle, Nika Sarraf; Missy Nelson; and Zoë Vorzimmer.

very vicious
should not be in
Library

Foreword to
Staccato Crime

A dozen years ago, my friend Allan Guthrie recommended to me an obscure crime novel from 1931, *Bodies Are Dust* by P. J. Wolfson. I immediately set out to find a copy, but there were none to be found anywhere in the vast universe of the internet. I turned to my local librarian for help, and she suggested I try the interlibrary loan network, which libraries use to borrow books from other libraries around the world.

As my librarian searched the interlibrary database for *Bodies Are Dust*, she arched her eyebrows and said, "It seems there only ten copies of the book in libraries worldwide."

I was similarly surprised and said, "That's fewer copies than the Gutenberg Bible," of which there were 49 in libraries and museums at that time.

"Of the ten copies," she added, "two of them are here in Austin."

When *Bodies Are Dust* arrived at my local library, I was thrilled to actually have a copy in my hands. As I opened the book I noticed someone had scrawled on the title page, "Very vicious—should not be in library." I laughed out loud. Flipping to the back of the book where due dates were stamped, I saw that it had been checked out many times in the 1930s and 40s, but the date stamped just above mine was March 27, 1948. No one had borrowed this book in over sixty years!

About the same time that Allan Guthrie was recommending *Bodies Are Dust* to me, my friend David Rachels (not coincidentally, the co-editor of this series) was also searching for a copy. Luckily, David found a 1952 paperback reprint that Gary Lovisi was willing to part with for less than fifty dollars. He and I have found that this is the case with too many outstanding crime books from the early twentieth century—if you're lucky enough to find a copy, you also have to be lucky enough to afford it.

As I write, there is one copy of *Bodies Are Dust* for sale on Amazon, eBay, or AbeBooks, and that copy is in French. When an English-language copy appears, it might be an affordable paperback (affordable, that is, if it is in tattered condition), or it might be an expensive hardcover ($800-$1000, depending on condition and whether it's a first or second edition).

Staccato Crime will solve this problem by publishing affordable paperback editions of difficult-to-find noir fiction and true crime from the Jazz Age, 1899-1939. Our hope is that when a friend recommends to you an obscure work of early twentieth-century American crime, you will be able to find a copy here—and also, that Staccato Crime will lead you to recommend these books to your friends.

Jeff Vorzimmer
Austin, Texas

New and Forthcoming Titles
From Staccato Crime

Introduction

"Nothing is terrible to me."
—Inspector Buck Safiotte

Pincus Jacob Wolfson was born on May 22, 1903, in a tenement in the Lower East Side of Manhattan. His Russian-immigrant parents aspired for their children to become professionals, so Wolfson took the quickest path he could see: a two-year pharmacy degree from Fordham University in the Bronx, where his family was then living. In 1926, he married Billie Marmon, and the couple moved to Binghamton, New York, where Wolfson bought a drugstore. The business failed, however, because Wolfson was distracted. He found medicine less interesting than writing.

The Wolfsons returned to New York City, and P. J. ("Pinky" to his friends) took a job in a drugstore near Madison Square Garden. While working the late shift, he finished his first novel, *Bodies Are Dust*. He said that he wanted to tell "the truth" about the world as he saw it, but he thought he could do better, so he stuck the manuscript in a drawer and kept writing. Eventually, his wife asked him how the novel was going, and he confessed that he was now working on his second. Billie was appalled that her husband was not seeking a publisher for his first, and she told him so on a regular basis. Eventually, P. J. wore down, and he decided to appease her by submitting to one publisher. Looking in the phone book, he liked the name "Vanguard Press."

Vanguard Press had been founded in 1926 with the mission of publishing nonfiction classics in affordable editions for the education of working-class Americans. This enterprise was funded with a $100,000 grant from the American Fund for Public Service, and when this money ran out, the press shifted to more commercial endeavors. Leading this new version of Vanguard was editor, half-owner, and socialist James Henle. A champion of free speech who took pride in discovering new writers, Henle was the perfect editor for Wolfson.

But Wolfson would not have been published by Vanguard without substantial luck. First, of course, was his fortunate choice of "Vanguard Press" from the phone book, but he needed more luck than just that. When his unsolicited manuscript arrived at the publisher, it landed in the slush pile at precisely the right moment to wind up in the hands of James Henle. Henle liked to dip into the slush for travel reading, and Wolfson's manuscript was among those he took on a train ride from New York to Washington, D.C. *Bodies Are Dust* so excited Henle that he telegrammed Wolfson from Washington to offer publication.

Vanguard published *Bodies Are Dust* in 1931. The front flap of the book's dust jacket describes the novel's plot in surprising detail—"spoiler" does not enter the American lexicon until 1971—before concluding, "Mr. Wolfson is an author of amazing power and virility. His style is terse, muscular, nervous, strong. It is patently modeled upon that of Mr. Hemingway, yet so thoroughly has Mr. Wolfson mastered it and so different is the material upon which he employs it, that his talent can in no sense be termed derivative." Or, as Vanguard's advertising campaign declared, "Wolfson isn't Hemingway. Wolfson is Wolfson."

Wolfson's "different" material is police inspector Buck Safiotte, whom the dust jacket compares to "an Oriental monarch of three thousand years ago," referencing both the power of a monarch over his kingdom and the distance that he has to fall. The novel's blunt first paragraph establishes tone with Safiotte comparing the streets of New York to sores festering with pus. The rest of his narration is somewhat more restrained, and he tends to reveal his own character without showing awareness that he has written anything remarkable.

One revelatory moment early in the novel arises from a conversation between Safiotte and his housekeeper, Myra, who must serve not only Safiotte but also the women he brings home. Unmarried Myra reveals that she has a "love-child," and Safiotte suggests that there are "institutions for such children." Myra smiles and tells him that he does not understand, and Safiotte comments to his readers, "Perhaps I did not, but I did know that scrubbing floors and waiting on loose women hurt." With Safiotte pivoting from Myra's physical to emotional pain, he reveals a surprising empathy that darkens his narrative. Elsewhere, Safiotte writes that "'the top' was always my end, and

12

I trampled everything under for that," but he is not a monarch on high, far removed from his subjects. He may be on top, but as he tramples, he is fully aware of the pain that he causes.

Safiotte's story ends with jazz. Prior to the novel's final page, its musical references are empty. When Safiotte plays piano for a moment, he does not describe the sounds that he makes. When he hears a radio playing, he mentions "music" and nothing more. At one point there is music from a saxophone, which a woman describes as "keen," but Safiotte professes to have no idea what she is talking about: "Maybe you have to be educated in a certain way to know which music was keen, I thought; that was the first time I had heard music called keen"—whereupon the music stops. But in the final two paragraphs of *Bodies Are Dust*, Safiotte mentions jazz four times. At the end of the penultimate paragraph, "The music of a jazz orchestra came to us. Jazz and tears and death. That was it: jazz and tears and death." And then, in the final phrase of the novel: "crying mixed with the jazz music." Safiotte's story ends darkly, but he hears music as if for the first time.

Wolfson was understandably surprised when Hollywood wanted to buy *Bodies Are Dust*. The novel was, in his words, "based on themes the movies simply aren't allowed to use," but "if Hollywood wanted to waste money like that it was okay with me." He went to his publisher's office where a contract from Universal Studios "about 150 pages long" awaited his signature. Out of curiosity, he read the whole thing: "Sure enough, there was a little paragraph toward the end of it, saying the deal was off if there was any censorship trouble. I knew there wouldn't be anything else but. So I told the Hollywood folks that I'd sign the contract, only if they'd scratch that clause out. And they did." Of course, *Bodies Are Dust* was never produced, but Wolfson went to Hollywood to become a scenario writer, which changed the trajectory of his career. In his first few years, he wrote screenplays for Universal, Paramount, MGM, and RKO. The New York City pharmacist was on his way to joining the Beverly Hills Tennis Club.

In 1939, Wolfson got his chance to direct, and the result was *Boy Slaves*, which the *New York Times* described as "a grim little melodrama of peonage on the turpentine farms of the South. It is an indignant document, an indictment . . . of modern-day slavers who charitably relieve county jails of the necessity of feeding homeless boys by offering them employment and then proceed to bind them, through token money, scrip, company stores and brute force, to a condition of hopeless serfdom." The *Times* went on to praise Wolfson for "not salv[ing] the public conscience either by a prologue or epilogue affirming that 'events herein depicted are fictional' or no longer are true. . . . Hollywood, for a change, is actually standing up on its hind legs and saying that something is wrong with the world." Wolfson himself said that *Boy Slaves* "stirs you up inside and makes you mad when you leave the theater. It doesn't do any preaching. It just tells the facts as they are." This was Wolfson's only chance to tell "the truth" on screen. He never directed again, and today his most recognizable screen credit is for writing the nostalgic musical-comedy-biopic *The Perils of Pauline* (1947).

Wolfson published four novels in rapid succession with Vanguard before Hollywood fully consumed his energies: *Bodies Are Dust* (1931—aka *Hell Cop*), *Summer Hotel* (1932), *All Women Die* (1933—aka *This Woman Is Mine* and *Three of a Kind*), and *Is My Flesh of Brass?* (1934—aka *Pay Her for Passion* and *The Flesh Baron*). Near the end of his show business career, Wolfson published a fifth and final novel, the paperback original *How Sharp the Point* (1959). Ten years later, he reported having a sixth novel in progress, but that never appeared.

P. J. Wolfson's last novel in print was *All Women Die* in its 1962 reissue as *Three of a Kind*. Thus, when Wolfson died in 1979, all of his books had been out of print for at least 17 years, and he likely thought that his work—his effort to tell "the truth" about the world—would be forgotten. But if he thought this, he was wrong.

David Rachels
Newberry, South Carolina

Sources

Information about P. J. Wolfson comes from three sources:
Frederick C. Othman's article "Censorship Forces Writer to Take
Up Film Producing" (Louisville *Courier-Journal*, 20 March
1939, sec. 1, p. 7); the list of facts in *Contemporary American
Authors* (Volume 5-8, First Revision, 1969); and, most
significantly, two posts by Jeff Pickle ("The P. J. Wolfson Story"
and "The Remarkable Story of *Bodies Are Dust*") that appeared
on his blog *wdors* in 2010. Pickle's posts are based largely on his
email correspondence with Wolfson's son, Michael. Information
about Vanguard Press comes from Guy Henle's essay "Vanguard
Press: Sixty-two Influential Years" (*Columbia Library Columns*,
November 1990, pp. 3-13).

"Do not appease thy fellow in the hour of his anger, and comfort him not in the hour when his dead lies before him, and question him not in the hour of his vow, and strive not to see him in the hour of his disgrace."

Ethics of the Fathers.

BOOK ONE

I

It was spring when I was transferred to the new post; yet, it was little like spring, but like late winter. In the streets, the sidewalks were covered with ice, pebbled by thaws and frosts following each other rapidly; and the roadway was polished in some places by shiny ice and in *other* places, where it was too thick for freezing, was covered with dirty mud; so that, when a truck slowly passed, the mud would ooze and slough along the sides of the tires like pus from a festered sore. Other times, when a wagon drawn by horses would pass, coming from the docks, the mud from under the horses' hoofs would spatter on the sidewalk.

From the windows of the station-house we could look into the Parochial school and nunnery on the other side of the street. That was only during the day, because at night there were no children in the school and the nunnery was dim, too: the shades drawn and only shadows on the shades.

The school was yellow and straight and the nunnery was, too. On both sides were Red apartment houses with cornices, and jutting out stones, and rusty fire-escapes. I looked often at the windows in the top-floor of the red house next to the nunnery, because I knew a whore who lived there. Finally, she moved. She said, because of the surroundings. It hurt her business.

When it was cloudy and rainy and the children were let out of school, dressed in long raincoats that came to their ankles, it seemed to me, from where I was, looking through the window streaked with clean stripes by the rain that ran down on the dirt, as though I stood on a great height looking down on grown people. The nuns looked like black giants standing over them.

From the side windows, we could see over the roofs to the purple grey Palisades on the far side of the river, because the ground sloped away from us to the river's edge. The river could not be seen, but you knew it was there, because of the whistle of the boats and the dark clouds of smoke from the stacks. Sometimes, in the sunlight, if the boats went out into the river far enough, we could see the stacks with yellow or red bands painted around the tops. It looked very nice against the brown and grey of the earth and rocks of the Palisades on the other side of the river.

There were pigeons that came out of the cornices of the red houses, when the sun shone, and fed on the oats in the manure on the roadway. They made their nests under the cornices of the red houses; not in the yellow nunnery or the Parochial school, which were too flat.

On top of the Palisades, we could see a green woods that came to the edge, and I knew that it went deep into the country until it changed to scrub and then rolling farmland, because I went that way when I left the city for a vacation. When I looked at them, I remembered when we were boys and went first by hot, crowded elevated railway and then cool, green-plushed railroad—the fare was a "holdout" on our parents; I took an added joy in making a "holdout," because I kept thinking there would be less for the priests—to a green island in the Sound off the city (we had the slum's madness for green growing things), where we dug for mussels and bathed and lay half naked on the grass and leaves. Then we built fires to dry by and to broil the fish which we had caught.

I remembered when Teeny and Danny and I went looking for wood for the fire and found two women lying close to each other in the grass. One woman talked to Teeny and asked him if he wanted to play in her garden, and he answered, if her garden could hold all three of us, we would play. Then suddenly the mussel-flats became mud and the water, muddy and oily on top; and I sensed around me the atmosphere that had come to me when I had stolen down a darkened hallway after a kimono-clad whore and her client; and before me was only the vision of two women with skirts open on the side lying in the grass.

We took them back with us to the others and went into the boats. Teeny and one woman came into my boat. We were dressed in bathing suits, and when Teeny stood up and the woman reached up and took a piece of seaweed which was stuck to the upper part of his leg, touching the flesh, he dove off and into the water. She looked at me and laughed, and I laughed, too.

After that, when they asked me to go, I did not see green fields and trees, but a woman with large healthy breasts and wide hips pushing out of the wet seaweed that clung to her. We did not see them again, so I stopped going and stayed in the city, and learned to use the call-houses and to laugh, instead of biting my teeth when I heard my mother and father who slept in the same room with me.

II

The usual thing happened the next election: we won. And I was promoted to Inspector; but I was disappointed, because I had expected more than that. I did not say anything and did not let them know in any way—Forrester was dead, and the rest had short memories—so, I went to the new station-house where I had a whole upper-floor to myself and had a man six feet tall for a civil-secretary who drank my liquor when I was out.

The new station-house was old to me, because I had been a lieutenant there. Nothing was changed except that I was Inspector. There was the same kind of desk-sergeant and some of the patrolmen and plain-clothes-men were the same ones; they were a little older, but the same. They all made believe they were glad to see me, but I knew they were not. I was on top and they were the same—"the top" was always my end, and I trampled everything under for that.

Later, I went out with "The Yid" to look over some of my territory, and I knew it from before; only, locations were moved around a little, and the houses were less whorey looking, and the streetwalkers were not so open in their trade. We saw one "pick up" an old man, and it was done so nicely that even we doubted and did not know if they were not old friends.

It was very nice here. I was glad, even if they had not made me Commissioner, that I had this territory. It was a very rich territory, because I saw speakeasies, many on each street, and also hotels, many on each street, in which I knew sporting-women lived. The theatrical district was in it, where all the gamblers and dope-peddlers and gunmen practiced their respective professions. I would be careful, but I would be rich, and also, I would be pleased because I could have the choice of the nicest women.

The streets were no longer broken up to build a subway and paved with cobbles where there was no building, but were smooth and wide, and many automobiles used them. There were traffic lights that winked red and green orders to the automobiles at night. The cars looked like automatic things that moved by mechanical control, except in the theatrical district, where it was so light from the many electric signs, that you could clearly see the drivers at the steering-wheels.

As we walked, I wrote the addresses of several places—speakeasies are so easy to find—to check against the list on the bulletin-board in the detectives' room. The list was a private one of suspected violations that was kept for them. Every address in the district was listed with the name of the owner and the suspected violation next to it. I knew that those who paid well were not turned in for the list; not because a detective keeps faith with the one who pays him, but because the other fellow might learn of it and take some of it away from him. I promised them, mentally, a good shake-up. I was going to get all of my share.

When we came back to the office on the top-floor and I took a bottle out of the desk drawer, I knew that my civil-secretary had been there before me, because the liquor had been up to the Bordeaux label on the neck of the bottle when I had taken the last drink, and now it was below the label.

I called him in and held the bottle before him. He looked from me to the bottle and back to me. It was a four-cornered, squat bottle with a long neck that looked pretty with its gold-and-black label. I took a whiskey glass from the desk drawer and poured the brown, thick, sweet-smelling brandy into it and motioned him to drink. He looked at me, then at the liquor. The light shone dully through it.

"Drink it," I said.

He lifted it to gulp it down.

"Sip it, you sap," I said, to him, and he sipped it.

"Like it?"

"Yes, sir."

"Good, isn't it?"

"Yes, sir."

"That's the last. From now on, stay out of my desk. Now, get the hell out of here."

He blushed and went out, and in a minute I heard his typewriter clicking, then stop. I looked out at him and he was with his chin cupped in his hand looking into space. When he saw me watching him, he blushed again and bent over his typewriter.

I drank a large glass of Crème de Cocoa, holding it first to the light so that it shone a warm brown, and then sipping it slowly, pausing between sips for its flavor. The Yid, without an invitation, took a glassful and drank it down.

"How d' you drink that sweet goo?" he said.

"Like sweet things."

"It's for women."

I drink for taste and not for the drink. That is why I cannot drink gin. It is a liquor that is made for Englishmen and Swedes and all the other cold peoples. When it is for liquor, my Italian side comes in front; and also, when I get drunk I am Italian, because I become sad and bitter, and I pity myself.

Being warm with the brandy, I remembered what I thought was an injustice to me.

"The damn bastards," I said.

The Yid did not say anything. He knew what I was talking about, because he was my confidant. Acting as my bodyguard, he knew almost everything. I did not need a bodyguard, but I liked him and kept him near me.

"And he and I and that Jew, Stein, went to every whorehouse in the city together. And many a time we had the same girl— now, he hands me a deal like this."

"Why didn't you get something on him so you could hold it over him, if you had such sweet chances?"

"Who'd think that damn mug would be Mayor, and that Forrester would die just before election?"

"He was old, and you knew it."

"Sure I knew it, but he didn't have to go off and die just when I had everything coming my way."

"I don't know what you're croaking about," The Yid said.

He could talk that way to me, because I liked him and babied him, and he always went where I went and saw me when I was without any official dignity.

"Why shouldn't I croak, when I was promised the Commissioner's job?—the damn, dressed-up, window monkey!"

"They jumped you to Inspector."

"From where you are, that's a lot. I want to be on top."

The liquor was heating me. I slapped the top of the desk with the palms of both my hands. "On top! On top! Nothing else! And, goddammit, nothing'll stop me!"

"Yeh?" said The Yid.

"Yeh," I said and drank some more.

It was warm in the room. I got up and tried to open the window, and it was jammed tight, so I put all my force to it and it banged open suddenly. The extra effort brought some of the sour, half-digested brandy up into my mouth. I spat it out through the open window.

The same pain was coming like a hot band tightening around the lower part of my chest. I stood, holding on to the frame of the window, and breathed deep breaths of fresh air, but the pain got worse. My knees shook when I walked across the room to the toilet, and when I hit the calf of my leg against the point of the open drawer, I did not feel the pain, because the one in my stomach was much more.

I was just able to close and lock the door, when the floor suddenly rose up to meet my face. I tried to crawl up it with my hands, thinking that the cessbowl would turn over and spill its contents over me. I reached the cessbowl over my head, gripped the edges with my hands and pulled myself up, so that I was on my knees before it, and, on my knees, I retched and vomited like a pregnant woman in her first months. After the vomit I felt better, so I put off going to the doctor.

III

The pain in my head woke me in the morning. It was dark in the room, because I sleep with the shades drawn down. Even when I am drunk, I do not forget to pull them down. I could not see what it was like outside. I went to the window and let up the shade, and the sun came through the window. The air coming through the ventilating-screen was cold, but I stood there with my head against the cold windowpane and looked across at the park. The trees were covered with frost that shone in the sunlight—it must have rained during the night for a frost to be on the trees.

While I looked out, the traffic-policeman stopped the automobiles, all of them shiny with nickel and bright colors, and a nursemaid pushed a baby-carriage across to the park. I went into the bathroom, held my head under a cold shower, shaved, dressed, and went into the hall.

A letter was on the small table and, as I opened it, a key rattled in the door-lock, the door opened, and Myra came in. She said, "good morning," and went into the kitchen to prepare breakfast for me, and looking at her, I forgot the note. She was my housekeeper. She made breakfast for me and stayed in my apartment until twelve, noon, cleaning the rooms. There was a friendship between us, but what kind, I did not know; for, friendships with women were with me for only one thing, and with her it was not so—so I did not know.

One time, when I noticed how straight her body was and how the smooth, firm skin and standing breasts hid the bigness of her nose, I put my arms around her and kissed her mouth a few times. She stood straight and stiff and became very white. It was like the night that I was very drunk in the Venetian Gardens and tried to kiss a statue. I was angry, but I let it pass by, because I did not want to lose a good housekeeper and mornings were hard and nasty tasting to me, anyway. I laughed at her white face. It was white like that when she would come in and find a lady with me and have to serve us.

She told me later that she had a child, a boy, and it had no father—she called it a love-child. The whole affair, as she told it, was strange; she was not sorry; and to me, a bastard was a bastard. I said as much, and also that she was young and had her whole life before her; there were institutions for such children. She only smiled and told me I did not understand. Perhaps I did not, but I did know that scrubbing floors and waiting on loose women hurt.

She looked up and saw me watching her.

"Been sick again," she said.

"Yes."

"When are you going to see a doctor?"

"Don't know. Sometime."

"You better see one soon. I know a man who waited too long and it was too late."

"I don't think it's bad."

"You don't get such attacks if it isn't bad. You better go."

"What's the difference?" I said. "Why should it worry you?"

"Don't behave like a boy. My little boy behaves like that sometimes."

"Does he?"

"He's cute—you don't like children?"

"Sure. I like Teeny's kids."

"That reminds me. Mr. Tinevelli called up yesterday. I left a note for you. It's on the hall-table."

"It's your note?"

"Yes. I left it. He wants you to come down."

"When?"

"Any time this week—you better eat. You shouldn't have bacon. It's fried stuff. That's bad."

"It's not that. It's the rot-gut you get for liquor."

"Whatever it is, promise you'll go see a doctor."

"Promise! Why should I promise you?"

"Because you're alone and somebody must take care of you. Maybe I want to mother you."

"Don't make me laugh. You should've seen my mother."

"Was she nice?"

"Nice! Jesus Christ! Was she nice! As nice as a tough Irish woman could be, married to a hair-trigger wop. I'm the result."

"You're not really bad."

"Going to try and reform me again?"

She became white.

"No," she said.

"Good," I said and got up from the chair and went into the hallway to get my coat.

On the street, it was cold and dry. There was a west wind blowing that meant it would stay clear for a while.

I stepped into the corner drug-store. My mouth was dry and the effect of the coffee I had drunk for breakfast was wearing off. The proprietor who knew me was behind the counter.

"Good-morning," he said.

"Morning. Give me a bromo."

"No good, Inspector. A chaser will do better."

"What have you got?"

"Gin."

"Hell, no!"

"Gibson's?"

"All right."

"Come in the back."

We went into the back room. He opened a drawer and took out a bottle of liquor from which he poured two glasses. We drank together.

"Another one?" he asked.

"No. If you have something sweet, I will."

"Not here. At home. Some good Benedictine. Come over some night when my clerk is here."

"Sure, I'll come."

"I want you to see my wife. My son, too. He's a big boy. Almost as big as you."

"All right. Some day. Well, good-bye."

I wanted to pay him, but he said it was on the house.

"Good-bye," I said.

I went out and around to the side street to the garage, and started up the steep driveway which ran to the first story, where my car was. I leaned against the grade walking up and it was like the night before, because the floor was coming up towards my face. Whether it was the suggestion or the bacon I ate, I did not know, but the pain was back. I turned around and went back to the drug-store.

"Give me something for a bellyache," I said.

"All right. I'll fix you up."

He took a square, yellow box out of a drawer and dumped a quarter of the contents into a glass; on top of that he poured a red liquid that smelled of bitter almonds.

"Elixir Bromides," he said.

"I don't give a damn what it is, so long as it stops it."

"It'll stop it. Get it often?"

"For the last six months."

He stirred the mixture, gave it to me and I drank it.

"When do you get it?" he asked.

"Right after I eat and right after I drink liquor."

"Doing something?"

"Yes."

"What?"

"I put my finger into the back of my throat and make myself vomit. After that, it relieves me."

"Maybe it's an ulcer?"

"Maybe."

"You ought to be x-rayed. Why don't you be x-rayed?"

I did not answer him, because I could not. The medicine was not doing me any good and I was getting nauseated again.

"You got a toilet here?" I asked.

"Yes. In there."

"I better use it."

I went in, and I came out feeling better, only for the taste of vomit in my mouth. He moved away from me a little, so I knew he smelled it.

"Give me something to rinse my mouth."

The mouth-wash he gave me was red and tasted of cinnamon.

"Why don't you get x-rayed?" he said again.

"Maybe I should."

"You really should. Here's an address—he's very good. And he's very reasonable."

"It isn't the money."

"I know. But you don't like to get robbed."

"No."

"Of course not! And he's very good. Go today."

"Not today. I can't go today."

"All right, tomorrow."

"Maybe, tomorrow," I said.

"I'll call him and tell him you're coming. He's a friend of mine, and if I tell him you are my friend, he'll treat you better. You don't want him to think you came in off the street."

"No. Call him."

I took the address and said "good-bye."

In the garage, I called The Yid by telephone and told him to be ready because I was coming downtown and would pick him up. He said that I had waked him, and that he would be ready.

The day got warmer as the sun came up higher. I drove along the street that runs along the edge of the park. The ice was melting off the trees, and the drops were like tears. It was very pretty. I liked it. After such pain, the relief felt good; even better than before there was pain.

I drove past the entrance of the park. There was a large statue of Columbus there and the icicles clinging to it were melting.

A policeman stopped the traffic, but waved me on when he saw the police-shield on the radiator. I drove down a side street and into a quieter avenue.

There was no place for me to park in front of the hotel in which The Yid lived, so I drove to a side street and walked back. It was a cheap hotel and it looked cheap. There was a long canopy outside with the name of the hotel on it, and the rest looked like a dirty apartment house. On the side was a bus-depot for out-of-town buses, and on the other side of the depot they were tearing down several houses to make the station wider. It was very dusty and dirty and smelled always of gasoline.

I went inside to get The Yid. The desk-clerk called his room. He would be down in five minutes; he was shaving, he said. I went out and walked to the corner for a paper.

"Know me, Monk?" I said to the newsman.

"Sure, Looey, sure!"

"You got a good memory. It's a long time."

"Don't never forget."

I knew him a long time. He was half-witted—no, not exactly half-witted, but he was not all right. He was dressed in a brown coat which was torn in shredded scallops at the bottom and came to his ankles. It was the same coat in which I had first seen him. A dirty grey cap was pulled low over his head, but it was not low enough to hide the uncombed grey hair. His eyes were sunk deep into his head; maybe it was the heavy, shaggy eyebrows that gave the impression of deepness. He was always sniffing, and his big nose was red from the many wipings. He held the rag in his fist and used an upward motion that showed his stretched nostrils; then, he would finish with a few sniffs.

"Making money, Monk?" I said.

"Pretty good, pretty good. Sometimes yes, sometimes no. I ain't here all the time, any more. I got a stand over near the sub. Only sell 'mornings' here."

"You happy, Monk?"

"Absolutely. Got no worries. Go to sleep every night. Got no worries."

"That's good. Give me an *American*."

He gave me the paper. I held out a coin to him.

"Don't want your money."

"Then I don't want your paper."

"Okey, Looey, okey," he said and took the coin.

From where I was, I saw The Yid come out of the hotel and look around. He saw me and came towards me.

"You look like hell," he said.

"I'm going to a doctor tomorrow."

"It's about time."

"I guess so," I said.

"Why don't you go to the hospital?"

"You know how they work. Why should I?"

"They wouldn't work on you like that," he said.

"To hell with them. I can pay a specialist."

"Maybe they know more."

"For Christ sake, wise up to them! Aren't you wise to them yet?"

"I thought . . ."

"To hell with them," I said.

We came to the car and got in. I backed out of line and started across to the East Side.

"I didn't eat yet," The Yid said.

"You can eat downtown."

"Where we going?"

"Tinevelli's."

"Maybe we better go to the 'house' first?" he said.

I turned the car around at the next corner and went back and saw Captain MacDunn. He was a Scotchman and as money-loving as all of them, and all of us. He liked whiskey, and he hated women. When there was a raid on a house and the boys took the girls up into the rest-room before locking them in downstairs, and he found out about it, he did not blame the boys, but went down into the cell-room, paced the corridor, and mouthed filth at the girls. We had reached an agreement, and he kept a personal and private record of how much was paid, and by whom. He kept this record in a code of his own invention.

I was not needed, so we started downtown again. I drove very fast. There was no heavy traffic on the East Side avenue. Soon we were in what was called the slums, and then "Little Italy"; and nothing was changed; and I still hated it. I went there only to visit Teeny. He had never left it; even when he studied and then got the idea of an Italian bank and organized and built it. He lived on "The Island," but he worked here where he had lived. He should have been a poet—he said everything was beautiful there. I saw only the dirt and it reminded me too much of my childhood.

There were the same pushcarts, the same rotting vegetables, and the same narrow streets. Dirt and stink and darkness were everywhere. It made me wonder what it was that made people leave a place of sun, laughter, and long life, and come to darkness and disease and be happy in it because they could see a motion-picture and wear silk stockings. (Silk stockings were everywhere, stepping among the rotting vegetables.)

We came to the bank. It was like a clean spot on a sore skin. In that, too, Teeny had to be sentimental. He had torn down the house in which my family and his and two dozen other families had lived and had built the white clean bank with tall windows and a high ceiling.

"I'm going to find a place to eat," The Yid said. "I'm hungry."

"Don't hold me up. I'm not staying long, and I don't want to wait."

"I eat fast."

He walked away and I went in through the revolving doors, trying to think of what it was the place always made me feel when I came in. I knew that I did not like the feeling.

There were no customers so early, and the tellers smiled to me and one said, "Hello." The special policeman said, "Hello, Captain." He had not heard about the inspectorship. That was what I meant. If I was Commissioner, he would have known.

Teeny was sitting at his desk when I walked into his office. He looked sick. He always had been thin and small and dark looking, but now he looked sick. His left eyebrow twitched every few seconds. He got up.

"What the hell's the matter with you?" I said.

"Nothing."

"You sick?"

"No."

"You look sick," I said.

"So do you."

"Well, I am."

"What's the matter?" He looked really concerned.

"Don't know yet. I'm going to see a doctor tomorrow and get x-rayed. I think you need it more than I do."

"I don't. What's the matter with you?"

"Stomach," I said.

"How is it?"

"Rotten. Vomit and pain and pressure over the heart."

"Why didn't you go before?"

"Shut up! What did you want me for?" I said to him.

He sat down at the desk, picked up the paper knife and poked holes into the green blotter. I sat down opposite him and waited for him to speak.

"Buck."

"Yeh?"

"I want you to draw your money," he said.

"What for?"

"For Christ's sake don't ask me stupid questions. Draw your money."

"What's up, Teeny?"

"Nothing. I don't want your money here," he said.

"That's no excuse."

"It's all the excuse you need. We don't want your account."

"Why?"

"It's dirty money."

"You're a liar. What's up, Teeny? You in wrong?"

He jumped up, banged his fist against the top of the desk; his face twitched, and he almost slobbered.

"Don't talk to me that way, you son-of-a-bitch. I don't want your dirty account in the bank," he shouted.

I knew Teeny, so I knew something was wrong and I was surprised and couldn't figure it, because he never gambled but played safe investments; and the bank was his whole life.

"Well?" he said.

"What do you want?"

"I told you."

"Why don't you tell me what's up. Want me to get out from under? That's it."

"I don't want your money in the bank." He said it quietly now.

"Why don't you stop that, Teeny, and come across? Maybe I can help."

"I don't want your money." He was getting excited again.

"Sit down. I'll take it out," I said.

He sat down, opened a drawer, and took a cheque-book out of it.

"Here, write a cheque for the full amount," he said, and handed me the book.

"Don't know the amount, I haven't my passbook."

"Here's the amount."

He gave me a slip of paper. On it was written an amount. I looked up at him and said: "Got it all ready, didn't you?"

"Write the cheque," he said.

I made out the cheque payable to myself.

Teeny pressed a button and, in a minute, one of the tellers came in. He gave the teller the cheque.

"Cash that," he said.

"Father MacLaughlin is outside, sir," the teller said.

"Father MacLaughlin?" I said.

"A friend of mine. Lay off, Buck."

The priest came in. He was tall and lean and iron-grey, and even his face was greyish. He wore the black skirt of the Jesuits and when he walked it flapped and swished like a woman's dress; but his walk was the walk of an athlete.

"Good morning," he said.

"Hello, Father," Teeny said and he became calm, and his eyebrow stopped twitching. He smiled. I did not like it because I did not like priests, and I could have done more for him, if he had confided in me.

"Father, meet Inspector Safiotte of the Police Force," Teeny said. "This is Father MacLaughlin. He is one of the professors at the University. I didn't have the luck to have him. He teaches anatomy."

I got up and we shook hands.

"You cut up bodies?" I asked.

"Yes."

"Women's bodies?"

"And little children's," he said.

"Yes?" I said and looked him in the eyes. They were grey, and I saw myself reflected in them. We looked at each other a little while.

"You don't like priests," he said suddenly.

"No."

"Why?"

"They're all liars."

"Liars? How?"

"A man is a man," I said.

"What do you mean?"

"Do they castrate priests?" I said.

"No."

"Then they're liars."

"When a man loves one thing and it is pure and true, he is a celibate to all others."

"What about the one who felt my old lady when my father was downstairs getting a loaf of bread to feed him."

"I'm sorry. The subject has become distasteful."

"Cut it out, Buck," Teeny said.

"It doesn't matter, Mr. Tinevelli. Priest baiting is as old as creation."

"Anyway," I said, "they're as money-hungry as everybody else."

"Cut it out," Teeny said. "Sit down, Father."

The priest sat down and arranged his skirt so that the cross was in full view of Teeny, just like a salesman does with his wares when he comes in to sell.

"You said Mr. Safiotte is on the force. Perhaps he can help you?" Father MacLaughlin said.

"Father!" Teeny said.

"I'm sorry. I did not mean to betray anything. I meant it for your good."

"Confessor, too," I said. "Maybe I could help him! Why should I? He don't even tell me about it."

The teller opened the door and came in.

"There isn't enough money to cover this, Mr. Tinevelli," he said. "I certified it, maybe the deposits will cover it."

"Leave it," Teeny said and took the cheque. He was white and he did not look at me, only looked down at the desk. The eyebrow was twitching again.

"You don't have to be so jumpy, Teeny. That's what I thought anyway," I said.

"What did you think?"

"Short accounts."

"You're all wet."

"All right, I'm all wet."

"You are."

"Why so anxious for me to be all wet. If everything was all right, you would only laugh."

"I am laughing."

"What a hell of a laugh!" I said, and I turned and pointed at the priest. "I'll bet he's laughing better than you are. Figure up all the dough you gave that bunch, and I'll bet it would get you out of this hole."

"Keep quiet."

"Ask him for it. Go ahead, ask him for it. You'll get it—in the pig's neck, you will."

"I cannot give that which is not mine to give," the priest said.

"There's your help for you, Teeny. There's your help for you."

"Shut up, dammit. Shut up, Buck," Teeny said, speaking loud.

I put the certified cheque down on the desk. The Yid opened the door from the outside and stood in the doorway, just as I put the cheque down.

"Here you are, Father," I said slowly and very quietly, "a contribution. Pimps and whores and gunmen chipped in to make it—now, refuse it."

"I cannot, but I certainly will include your remarks, and I am almost certain it will be returned."

"Bunk," I said and took up my coat. "Beg pardon, Yid, meet Father MacLaughlin."

"Shalem Halachem, Shammes," The Yid said.

"Halachem Shalem," the priest said.

When I went through the bank to the door, it suddenly came over me what it was I did not like about it; it was too much like a church.

IV

The next morning, I went to the doctor. His office was in a hotel and had a private entrance off the street and a sign "walk in" on the door. Two girls were sitting on the window seat with their legs pulled up under them. They were smoking cigarettes. The doctor was in his pajamas and was very embarrassed. He explained that he had not expected me. Only by appointment. Did not have an appointment. Very sorry to be this way. Would I wait? The maid should not have left the door open that way. Sorry to make such an impression. They were some near relatives. I said it was all right and that everybody, even doctors, were human. He said "human," as though he did not understand. Near relatives staying with him. Would I wait till he was dressed? I said, hell, yes.

I sat in a fancy Spanish chair with a narrow back and studded with fancy pointed, brass studs. It was very uncomfortable. I could feel the studs pushing into my back. It made me restless. It was hot in the room, and I thought, if the girls would get off the window seat I could open the windows. I tried to keep my mind off the heat by interesting myself in the decorations. It was pretty, all Spanish: banners, spears and old brass-studded furniture, old rugs on the stone floor, and an iron and stone staircase to the next floor. I thought, this racket is as good as mine, and it is prettier than my place but, by God, I bet mine cost me more.

The doctor called me upstairs, and it was like going into a hospital. Everything was white and cool.

"Sit down," he said.

I sat down, holding my hat and coat in my lap.

"What's the trouble?" he asked.

I told him, starting from the beginning of the pain and sick feelings. He asked questions. How long? Did I feel hungry often? Did it pain when I felt hungry? Did the pain leave after I had eaten? What kind of pain was it and how long did it last and how long after I ate did it come? Did I smoke or drink? How old was I? Come inside here.

We went into another room. It had dark walls and furnishings and had no windows.

"Take your clothes off," he said.

I took my coat, vest, shirt, and undershirt off and began to unbutton my pants.

"Nevermind the trousers. Just leave them open so that the buttons won't be in the way. Get between this and this."

I stooped and stood up between a big black box and a mirror swinging on an arm. I supposed it was a fluoroscope machine. That was the first time that I saw one.

The doctor went behind a screen, started a motor and put out the lights. He sat down in front of me. The hum became a crackle and his face was lit up by a dim bluish light, and I felt a prickle along my back where it rested against the machine. He pushed my stomach hard with his hands, which were covered with heavy rubber gloves.

"You didn't eat anything this morning," he said.

"No. The girl who cleans my house said that you shouldn't eat when you go to a stomach doctor."

"Good girl," he said. "We can start with the 'series,' now."

He put the lights on and switched off the motor and the hum died down. He went out and came back with a glass of white thick stuff.

"When I tell you to drink this, drink it slowly. Stop when I tell you to."

He gave me the glass, put the motor on and the lights off again. Blue light and prickles again. Drink it, please. Slowly, please. Stop. A little more, now. Stop. All right. Lights again.

Then, on a table, with metal plates pressed against my stomach. Hold your breath. Buzz. All right. Turn on your side. The right side, please. Hold your breath. Buzz. All right. You may get dressed.

I had to back off the table because my pants were down below my hips and I could not use my feet to get off sideways. I kicked over what was left of the white stuff while I was getting off and the maid had to be called in from outside to mop it up; she did not look pleased about it.

"All right, Inspector Safiotte—that's the name, isn't it?" the doctor said. "Come back in six hours and don't eat or drink anything—not a thing!"

When I went downstairs to go out, the girls were no longer there.

The second time, it was the same thing; only, I did not have to drink anything. He told me, before I left, that I could eat anything and to come back in the morning.

I walked up the stairs of the station-house. The building was old and the paint on the bricks was peeling off in flakes; it matched all the rest of the houses in the immediate neighborhood. It was a hole; and I thought of the Commissioner's office.

I went through the door. The man on door-duty saluted me with the sloppy salute that all policemen have. I did not return his salute, but passed into the desk-room. The desk was built like a judge's stand on the extreme left of the room; and now there was a group in front of it. Someone was being charged. There was plenty of loud talking.

The desk-sergeant called to me when I turned to the right to go up the stairs to my office.

"What do you want?" I said.

"This bird here says he wants to see you."

I went over.

"Jees, lemme talk to you!"

I looked closely; it was "Big Stem James," older, but the same "Big Stem"; a familiar figure on the "Big Street"; a man who had gone through several fortunes; a "dope" addict. The last I had known of him was that he was "running" tickets for a ticket speculator. With him was another addict of whom I knew.

"In again, 'Big Stem'?" I said.

"For Chrissakes, it's not scalping this time. Lemme talk to you."

"He's a god-dammed thief, a lousy son-of-a-bitch of a thief," the other man said.

"What're you in this?" I said.

"Makin' the complaint—the god-dammed thief."

"Bring them upstairs," I said to the policeman.

We went upstairs. I first, and the rest of them following, making a clatter on the wooden steps.

The Yid was sitting at my desk when we walked into the office.

"Where you been all day?" I asked.

"Tell you later, sir," he said, nodding towards the others. He was very respectful when there were others around. That was why I liked The Yid; he showed he had sense.

I sat down.

"Now, one at a time. James, you first."

"Tell the copper to get out and I'll tell it straight," he said.

"Get out," I said to the patrolman, and he went out.

"I don't have to kid you, Cap."

"Inspector!" I said.

"Inspector—you know I'm on the stuff and he's on it. His 'pusher' got pneumonia, and he couldn't get any, so he comes to me and says, here's a hundred and get me a hundred's worth of stuff. I asks him what kind he uses, and I goes out and gets it for him. He uses some and he's satisfied. I dunno what he wants."

"He's a liar," the other said. He was tapping his foot and drumming his fingers on the desk and shifting from foot to foot.

"Shut up!" I said. "Go ahead, James."

"Three o'clock in the morning, he comes bangin' on my door, tearin' his hair and claimin' it was crap. The noise he was makin'! I ducks him till this afternoon. He sees me on the street and the sap goes and has me picked up, even if *he* has to go in for dopin'. Lissen, Cap . . ."

I did not correct him that time.

"Don't put me away. You know I got a weak heart and I'll pass out in the pen. I give him the stuff, just as sure as he's born, I give him the stuff!"

"He's a god-damned liar. It was milk sugar."

"Keep quiet, you, 'Smirker,'" I said. "James, come across." I saw that he was burning with narcotic and that the other was burning for it.

"So help me, that's the truth!"

"Open up," I said.

"What else?"

"You tell me."

"I did."

"Not all of it," I said.

"The dirty son-of-a-bitch," 'Smirker' said.

"Shut up, you lousy dopey," James said.

"I'm a dopey! Why—you lousy—"

"You two, shut up! Now, James, come across or I'll call the cop in and you settle it downstairs." I said.

"All right, Cap. I got into a crap-game and lost the dough and had to give him milk sugar."

"Levinson," I said to The Yid, "frisk him."

"All right, all right, Cap. Here you are," James said and took a cigarette packet out of his pocket and threw it on the table.

I knew immediately, from his hurry, that he had a gun on him.

"Smirker" made a motion towards the packet, but I covered it with my hand. He stood over me, his lips jerking back into a smirking grin, his fingers drumming on the desk.

I took a sheet of paper out of the desk and tore it into two pieces and divided the contents of the packet into as nearly two equal parts as I could.

"One for each," I said. "And one chirp out of you, 'Smirker,' and you make an appearance under your own name."

His yellow face became grey. He picked up his share and went out of the office, almost running in his anxiety to get to some place and recharge himself with the narcotic.

James picked up his share.

"You got a rod on you, James," I said.

"So help me, Cap . . ."

"You got a rod," I repeated deliberately.

"Lissen, I got something for you. Forget about the rod. It's a big chance to make a killin'."

"Spill it!"

"Nothing doin'," he said and looked at The Yid.

"Go outside," I said to The Yid, and he went out.

"You want to make a killin'?"

"'Big Stem,' I know you a long time and you know me and. . . ."

"Yeah! Remember the time you brought a broad up to my room, in the middle of the night, and I had to sit out on the fire-escape?"

"Let that pass."

"Sure. Only—what a load of diamonds that dame had!"

"I said, let it pass. Go ahead with the story."

"Okey, Cap. The Stadium fight is goin Tierney's way. It's fixed."

"Old stuff. How d'you know?"

"Nevermind. Lay every buck you got."

"It don't have to be fixed; it's going his way anyway. Slater's through."

"Maybe. Only, the refree's gonna give it to him win or lose."

"How about a knockout?"

"Foul."

"Who's fixer?" I said. "Before I bet, I have to know."

He looked at me closely.

"What you feedin' me, Cap?"

"What the hell do you mean?"

"Don't *you* know?"

"Cut that."

"Christ—you and him being friends, I thought you knew. I only told you because you'd think I was tellin' you things and wouldn't be too tough. Don't let on I told you, or the finger'll be on me in a minute."

"Who're you talking about?"

"The Boss."

"Who, Levines?"

"No. I ain't workin for them anymore."

"Who're you working for?"

"Stein. Mike Stein."

"Stein?"

"Yeh, your friend. That's why I thought you was in on it. Don't give me away, Cap."

"You sure?"

"Yep. That's why I took the mug's century. Think I need his dough? All my money is down."

"Since when is Stein in on this racket?"

"Where you been? Stein and Wallace is like this." He crossed his index and middle finger. "He showed Wallace how to make money out of the ticket racket from inside; now, they're pals. He got a slice of the Stadium stock, and everything. That's how come he got to bettin' and refree fixin'."

"All right, James. You keep the gun. Only, you better watch out somebody don't nab you and I'm not around."

"Don't worry. Ain't nobody gonna take me in. I went this time because I knew you was here and you don't forget. If I get nabbed for anything you can't get me off of, nobody's gonna take me in. This," and he tapped his heart, "wouldn't last a week without the stuff. I just as soon pass out and take a few coppers along as go nuts and bust myself against a stone wall."

"What are you up to, James?"

"Dunno what you mean."

"You know what I mean. You never toted a rod. Running tickets don't call for it. You got another iron in the fire."

"Nothin', you're all wrong."

"Well—like I said before—you know me a long time, but if I nab you for something dirty, you're going to come across through the nose or go in."

"Me, I'll never go in. Maybe on a slab."

"I got my eyes on you."

"I'm lily-white. Well—better be goin'. Bet all you got."

"Maybe."

"You're smart, you got to know for sure."

"You can bet on that."

"It's sure, Cap. Only . . ."

"So there is an only."

"Well . . ."

"Well what?" I said.

"If they find out about that kid."

"Who're 'they' and what 'kid'?"

"That damn bastard is running around with a minor," he said.

"What?"

"A minor. A kid. She ain't more'n fifteen."

"What!" I said and pushed him against the wall.

"Sure thing. I ain't lyin. A lot a guys knows it. The goddam fool! Smart, and a lousy little kid makes a monkey out of him. If the opposition hears it, good night!"

"The opposition?"

"Yeah. Since he's runnin' with Wallace, they got the whole sport-world down on 'em; specially, Connors, boss of the Purple Socks and Slater's manager, Willis. If those birds nab him, they're out in the cold."

"Who knows about it?"

"All the guys in the Agency. She comes around and uses the phone, and says, 'Hello daddy, can I have a ten-spot,' and like a shot, one of the boys is called over and told to give it to her."

"Where's he take her?"

"Hotels."

"Damn fool," I said.

"Yeah. If they get hep, good night!"

"I want her name and address, 'Big Stem.'"

"You ain't givin' me away?"

"Get going."

He went out, and The Yid came in.

"Who's 'Smirker'?" he asked.

"Don't bother me now," I said.

"He sure got white."

"He should. He's Mrs. Holland's brother."

The Yid whistled.

"The money that dame spent on him," I said. "He took the cure a couple of times, but he goes back on it. Poor sap. His wife went away with an army officer; brooding about it, he went to booze. A bartender put him on the stuff. Goddam women, anyway!"

"I was out today and made a date for us."

"To hell with your date."

"Nice girls."

"Don't bother me."

"My cousin came down from up-state with them. They dance in a vaudeville act. Nice girls, not bums."

"All right. We'll go."

"How'd you make out with the doctor?"

"Don't know. Got to go back tomorrow morning."

"They're nice girls," he said.

"Yeh?"

"No bums."

V

The Yid and I got out of the taxicab in front of the Hotel Holden. It was a new hotel and, like all the new hotels which did not charge much for rooms, it was a place where traveling salesmen and refined prostitutes could carry on their business with an air of luxury.

We went inside; tapestry hangings, plush chairs, women sitting with crossed legs, men wearing long, pointed, soft collars and big knotted ties.

"Nice girls," I said.

"They're nice girls. My cousin has a room here. They don't live here."

"Where do they live?"

"They got a furnished apartment around the corner. They're nice girls."

The elevator took us up to the fourth floor. We walked along the narrow hall to the last door and The Yid knocked. Someone said, "Come in," and we went in.

Two girls were sitting on the beds. One, a blonde, was smoking. The Yid's cousin was sitting in a rocking-chair. He rocked himself slowly back and forth. The Yid introduced me as Mr. Smith. It was the same game, and the girls knew it was not my name.

"Glad to know you, Mr. Smith;" and they said it with a knowing accent. Fine start, I thought. I was beginning to feel sorry that I had come; my mind was taken up with what I had learned that afternoon.

The girls were very young. The Yid tallied a lot, and his cousin did not talk enough, only rocked back and forth. He was big, and thin, and his legs stretched out of the low rocking-chair. His hands were knobby, the knuckles sticking out. The bottle of rye whiskey on the dresser had been half full when we had come in, and he emptied it with his continuous drinking. Reach up, take a drink, put it back, rock up and back, do not say anything; then, the process over again.

"Let's go," Blondey said.

We pushed out the lighted cigarettes and put on our hats and coats. The cousin did not want to go; got a cold, don't want to go. "Aw, Honey," the blonde said and kissed him. Don't want to go, damn.

"Come on, Pete," The Yid said.

Pete got up slowly and put on his hat and coat and went out into the hall. The Yid and I, because we were gentlemen, stepped aside while the girls went first, and I wondered if, after all, we were not the fools.

In the taxicab—we hired a cab to go around the corner— Pete sat between the girls and did not talk, only looked ahead of him as though he was not really there.

When we stopped in front of a delicatessen store and The Yid and the blonde girl went out to buy provisions, the dark one asked me what I did.

"Sell," I said.

"Sell what?"

"Cigars."

Pete moved and looked at me. I leaned over and shut the door and the light went out.

The Yid and the girl came in, and I smelled the garlic from the provisions. I decided not to eat or drink anything. I knew that I would be sick if I did.

The parlor in the apartment was being used by another girl; she had a man with her. We went into the kitchen; the girls took our hats and coats, hung them on hooks behind the door, and then began to cut bread for sandwiches.

"None for me," I said.

"Why not?" Blondey said.

"Doctor's orders."

"Sick?"

"Stomach."

"Poor boy. What is it?"

"Don't know yet," I said.

"Have some tea, anyway."

"Make it tea."

The tea and sandwiches were made. We sat around the kitchen table. Pete sat on the washtub, his legs reaching to the ground, his arms just long enough to reach the bottle of Gordon's gin on the table.

"Where you girls from?" I said.

"Salt Lake," the dark one said.

"Where's your home, Blondey?"

"Have no home. Maude's home is mine."

"You said it!" Maude said.

The blonde girl had beautiful hair. It was a golden yellow and she wore it straight back and in a knot on the nape. It shown in the light and kept attracting my eyes. She was not very good-looking.

"Beautiful hair," I said.

"Like it?"

"It's nice, real nice," I said, thinking that I would sleep with her because of her beautiful hair and wondering what the other two would do about splitting over Maude.

The girl of the parlor ran past the kitchen door pushing her man before her. We heard him retching in the bathroom. They came back and the girl looked in and apologized.

"I don't know what got into Bill; he never was sick before," she said and went back to the parlor.

The music of a phonograph came into us from the parlor. Blondey got up and did a tap-dance. She stopped while the music played and listened intently to a variation which was being played by the saxophone.

"Boy, that's keen. Isn't that keen?" she asked me.

I did not know, but I said it was keen. Maybe you have to be educated in a certain way to know which music was keen, I thought; that was the first time I had heard music called keen.

The music stopped and the girl sat down.

"You're not a Jew?" Blondey said to me.

"No."

"I like Jew-boys," Maude said.

"I don't," Blondey said.

"Why?" I asked.

"Because they're not fair."

"How?"

The Yid ready to scrap, also said, "How come?"

"They'll never break in a Jewish girl and they think it's smart and funny to break in a Gentile girl."

"That's not it," The Yid said.

"The hell it isn't," Blondey said.

"No. It's because the Jews are so close together that every Jewish girl is like a sister."

"We leave the breaking in to you Christians, and then we possess them," Pete said.

"You're a bunch of rats," Blondey said. She was getting a few drinks into herself.

Pete spoke again: "Rats! For every one we break in there's ten of you broken in by your own."

"That's a lie! A Jew-boy broke me in," she said.

"Did you cry and holler?" The Yid asked.

"No."

"What're you complaining about?"

"You don't get me," said Blondey.

"The hell I don't," The Yid said.

"He broke me in."

"Sure."

"Aw, hell!"

"I like Jew-boys," Maude said. "They tell you they love you; kiss you; play with you, you know it's a goddam lie, but it makes you feel good."

"I been in love," Blondey said.

"I never was," Maude said.

Pete spoke: "Was it any different?"

"Jesus Christ—was it different! He treated me like I was a lady."

"I never was in love," Maude said.

"Jesus Christ—love!" Blondey said.

"Jew-boys try to love you. I sometimes think they do it so you show them a better time," Maude said.

"The damn rats!"

"They're not rats," I said.

"Would you marry a Jew-girl if she'd been broken in by a Christian?" Blondey asked me.

"I would if I loved her," I lied.

"There are no Christians," Pete said. "No Christians among the Gentiles or the Jews."

"Hear, hear," Maude said.

"Men try to take it away from women and it isn't a matter of creed. It's just the pleasure of taking away something that is precious to someone else. If there was something of greater value, man would want that."

"A crook don't break into a safe because he wants the door. He wants what's inside," I said.

"The door is only a symbol. I used it as a symbol," he said.

"I don't understand."

"If you don't, I can't explain it."

"I don't. I know this; if she don't want to, she don't have to; if she wants to, she gets as much out of it."

"So? Look at her! She doesn't care. She likes to sleep with a man and no charge; and yet she cries to Jesus Christ for affection and to be treated like a lady. Is she robbed?"

"Shut up, Jew-boy, shut up!" Blondey said.

"It works the other way too. Isn't it funny that you seldom get 'a dose' from a paid harlot, only from one who's pleasure bent."

"You insinuating anything?" Blondey said.

"No."

"Better not. We're clean."

"I know it."

"Then lay off that angle; it's disgusting."

"No end, a cycle with no end. We breed, and it starts all over again without us; the same larceny," he said.

"You're drunk," Blondey said. She was very drunk herself.

"You're a bolshevik," The Yid said.

"How do you know I like it?" Blondey said suddenly.

"Here we are, kidding each other, and all the time, we're thinking; when does it start; what the hell's all the talk about; when do we get what we came for; what is he or she going to be like, and to hell with him or her afterwards."

"Is that so?" Blondey said.

"Isn't it?"

"Get the hell out of here, you damn Jews," she screamed.

"Keep quiet!" Maude said.

"I won't shut up! Get the hell out of here!"

"You better," Maude said. "She's drunk."

"I'm not drunk."

I felt very embarrassed. The yellow hair was no longer attractive. We took our coats.

"You can stay," Blondey said to me, and she put her arm under mine.

"I think I better go with them," I said. They were standing at the door looking back at me.

"Aw, stay."

"No. I came with them."

"Let the Jews get out; you stay."

"No. Good night."

We went out.

"I'm awfully sorry," Pete said drunkenly.

"That's all right," I said.

"What now?" The Yid said. "I'm excited enough to jump you two."

"Let's go over to the Princely Hotel. I know a couple of Gypsies there," I said.

"Gypsies! Let's go," The Yid said. "Say, that dame reminded me. I want a few days sick leave."

"What for?"

"I'm going up-state and marry this guy's cousin—cousin on his father's side."

I stopped and looked at him and said: "What the hell for?"

"It's about time," he said.

"Is that a reason?"

"Sure. I know how you feel about getting married, Chief. It's all right to run around, but a man's got to settle down some time. It's kind of different."

"If you'd slept in the same room with your father, a dirty wop, and your old lady, you'd know it's the same and no different."

"A duet played on a bedspring," Pete said. "Let's go to the Princely."

VI

It turned cold that night and then warmer. In the morning it began to snow. The snow came down in large flakes, like feathers, floating down because there was no wind. It was as though a feather-bed sky had been slit and the feathers allowed to sift down. In a few minutes the park and trees and walls were covered with it.

I sat at the window, looking out. The steam-radiator was close to the window, so that I was very comfortable. It was seldom that I felt well in the morning, and this time, perhaps, it was because I was not getting over a drunk.

I sat and did not think about anything, only watched the snow. Soon, I heard Myra come in and heard the rattle of dishes, and then she came into the bedroom.

"What did he say?" she said.

"Who?"

"The doctor."

"Don't know yet. Have to go back this morning. It don't worry me."

"I was worried."

"Why should *you* worry? It's my stomach."

"That's just it," she said.

"What's just it?"

She did not answer, only stood still, looking out of the window.

"Pretty, isn't it?" she finally said.

"Yes. And when it's walked on it'll be dirtier than if it wasn't there in the first place."

"It's beautiful, now—what will you do if the doctor tells you that you have a cancer?"

"I don't know."

Again there was a silence. I had to say something.

"How's your boy?" I said.

Her face lighted up. "He's fine."

"How old is he?" I did not care, but I was feeling good and wanted to say something that would please her.

"He's seven."

"You're not very old."

"I'm twenty-six."

"You were pretty young."

"Yes, I was pretty young."

"What was it, the country girl and the city guy?" I knew she was from the country.

"No. The boy next door."

"Wouldn't he marry you?"

"Why should he? He got what he wanted. He went away."

"He had to come back some time. You could've made him."

"I didn't want to."

"Why."

"Because of his father. He was old—over eighty—and full of pride; a member of the Legislature and fought in the Civil War. It would have broken his heart. I loved him."

"His life was over."

"Yes, it was over. That's why. . . ."

"You women! You love his son?"

Silence, then: "In a way."

"What did you do?"

"I went to his brother—he was in touch with him—and told him to write and tell him to come home, that I was going away. He said that it was fine because he had already made arrangements to have several other boys say that . . ." and she stopped.

"Nice boys," I said.

"I didn't care about that. Everybody knew we went together for years, and I didn't believe that they could get anybody to swear. I went because of the old man."

"How about the old man?"

"He's dead now."

"Funny! He died anyway."

"Yes. But I'm glad it's this way," she said and turned and went back to the kitchen.

I dressed and sat down to a hearty breakfast. The doctor had told me to eat anything, so I ate a full meal.

"Will you call me up and tell me what he says?" Myra asked.

"If I think of it," I said.

The doctor took only one "picture" and used the fluoroscope. He thought he had his finger on the trouble, he said. Took another picture to make sure. Would I come back in half an hour or did I want to wait in the waiting-room. He would develop the "picture." I said I would come back and went out and sat in the car.

I was not worried, one way or the other, but I did want to know what it was and get it over with.

A horse slipped and fell in the snow. I watched their efforts to get him back on his feet. They put ashes and burlap bags on the snow so that his steel shoes would grip, and finally, after heaving up and slipping a few times, they had him up again.

The half hour was up. I went back into the office and was called upstairs by the doctor. He switched on some lights behind ground-glass plates and put the negatives on them, so that the light went through the negatives. The one he had taken that morning was still wet and in a steel clip so that it would remain erect and not curl.

"Here's the first one," he said. "You see, absolutely normal stomach. No spots; absolutely clean, normal stomach. Now—here's the one taken six hours later. Stomach empty, and Barium Sulphate is in the lower intestines—that's the white mixture you drank. Now look at this. That's the appendix. See how it curls up and around. I tried to straighten it under the fluoroscope but couldn't. I moved it but couldn't straighten it. Evidently, it is adhered. Also, look at the obstruction."

He pointed to a dark spot on the appendix.

"I took another picture to make sure. Sometimes it's the fault of the x-ray, but you see the same condition. It's a chronic appendicitis in a very bad form. It'll have to come out soon. Take your coat and vest off again."

I took them off.

"Lie down here, please."

I climbed up on the table. He opened my pants, felt and measured a few inches from the hip-bone, towards the navel, and with all ten fingers pressed full force into my stomach. It hurt a little. Then, he suddenly let go and let the flesh snap back, and I thought my "gut" would not stop at the skin but would fly out of me and follow his fingers and I arched up and dropped back.

"Hurts, doesn't it?" he said.

"Yes."

"Just as I thought. Put on your clothes."

I put on my clothes and sat down near the desk. He was writing on a filing-card.

"You'll have to have it out right away," he said.

"I don't know."

"The sooner it's out, the better."

"I don't know. I'd have to see about it."

"I could get you Doctor Herbert; he's Director of Surgery."

"Yes?"

"He teaches the other surgeons."

"Yes?"

"If I sent you, he wouldn't charge you much."

"It isn't that. I would have to arrange things first."

"Let me know."

I got up. What should I do in the meantime? I was feeling pain from his pressing my stomach.

"There's nothing you can do. If you feel pain, use an ice-bag; never use heat. It'll act up sometimes and you'll vomit. You can't prevent that."

"How much do I owe you?" I asked.

He handed me a bill. It was for two hundred dollars. I made out a cheque.

Downstairs, I sat down for a while in a chair. The pain was getting worse. It was as though someone was snapping an elastic-band regularly against my skin, and when I got up, I could not straighten myself and had to crouch a little.

Myra let me in. Her hand went to her mouth, and then she grabbed my arm.

"What is it?" she said.

"Nothing."

"What did he say?"

She thought that I was sick because of what the doctor had told me. I explained to her. She wanted to help me undress, but I told her to get the hell out and buy some ice. She said there was ice in the box and went out to buy the ice-bag. I undressed and put on a pair of pajamas and got into bed.

Presently, she came back. She was out of breath. I knew she had run to the drug-store and back, and I felt grateful and a little ashamed at the pleasure I had taken in hurting her with my women.

Under the ice-bag, the pain changed from a snapping to like mice eating away at my insides, and then to numbness. When the bag had to be refilled and was removed, the pain would start up again and then die out when the bag was back.

I dozed, and once Myra changed the bag and dried my stomach where the bag had leaked a little. I felt it in a kind of outside-of-myself way, because I was more asleep than awake. It was very nice in bed. Never enjoyed being in bed; but now it was nice. Dream and drift away into nothing.

Somebody was shaking my arm, and it was hard to bring myself back.

"Buck, open your eyes!"

"What's the matter?"

"Thank God! You were hardly breathing. I'm going to call the doctor."

"What for? I'm all right now; I feel fine."

"I'm going to call him. What's his name and address?"

"I don't need a doctor. I feel good."

"What's his name and address?"

I told her, and she went to the telephone in the hallway. I heard her call information and get her number. Would he come right away? Yes, very sick. Pain, ice, low pulse. Right over? She called another number. Won't be home. Give the baby supper and put him to bed. Maybe late, maybe not all night. Sick, very sick. Good night.

"What time is it?" I asked her when she came back into the bedroom.

"Seven."

"Night, already?"

"Yes."

"You been here all day. Why don't you go home?"

"Leave you?"

"I'm all right," I said.

"The doctor is coming."

"I don't need a doctor."

"You don't know how sick you are."

"I feel all right."

She did not answer me, but went to the window and looked out.

"Still snowing?" I said.

"Yes. It's still snowing." Her voice sounded "sing-song."

"It's tough on the horses," I said.

The doctor uncovered me, and I pulled the cover back over the top of my legs and he pulled it down again absent-mindedly. I looked at Myra and saw that she was seeing only his fingers measuring, so I let the cover stay.

The pain came back suddenly when he pushed.

"I knew it would be soon, but not as soon as this," he said.

"You're pushing," I said.

"That sometimes happens when it's bad. I'll call a private ambulance and have you over to the hospital. I think I can get Doctor Herbert for you. He doesn't like to operate at night; but if it's necessary . . ."

"Do you have to cut?" Myra said. "Can't you freeze it?"

"It's too late now. There's nothing to worry about; it's a simple operation."

"There're always complications."

"Nonsense, Mrs. Safiotte!"

She blushed. "I'm not Mrs. Safiotte."

"Pardon me," the doctor said and turned to me. "Did you vomit?"

"Yes, my breakfast."

"Good," he said. Then, to Myra: "Give him an enema— where's the phone?"

Myra showed him where the telephone was.

The ambulance-men were not very gentle. They must have been hardened to their work. I guess it was like anything else. They rolled the blanket around me and put me on the stretcher.

Myra put on her hat and coat. The doctor had gone away after he had made arrangements by telephone. We went outside, rang for the elevator and it came up. The elevator was too narrow, and we had to go down the steps; I on the stretcher and Myra walking behind. On the landing, we had to stand aside; two men were carrying a radio upstairs and blocked the stairway.

When we came out on the street, Myra pulled the blanket over my face. I felt the stretcher being lifted and pushed on a slide. I pushed the blanket away from my face. We were in the ambulance.

The motor started. The wheels spun around in the snow, the chains making a ringing sound, and then suddenly the wheels gripped, so that the ambulance started with a jerk.

It was like riding in a lower berth in a train, only it swayed and bumped more. We were going uptown. Every time we passed a light, I could see Myra's face; she looked very cold. I thought it was warm. Maybe, the blanket made me warm.

We bounced a lot over a cobbled street. The elevated-railway pillars flashed past; we were traveling under it. The driver made a left turn and went up a steep incline. It was so steep that I began to slip down the stretcher, and my feet pushed up against the end of the shelf, and I did not slip anymore; but Myra put her arms around me and held me. She did not know that I was holding myself. I could feel her breasts and her heart beating, and her face was near mine. She looked at me and kissed me.

"What's the idea?" I said. "I'm not dead yet."

She let go of me and sat back; the car had come to a stop in the yard of the hospital.

The hospital was built on a high shelf of rock off the street—it was that incline we had gone up. All I could see of it from the side windows of the ambulance was a red wall, a high pile of pea-coal, and some bare tree branches which the wind snapped against the windows of the ambulance. They were like thin, old fingers scratching on the glass.

The men lifted me out, and this time Myra had no time to pull the blanket over my face, and the snow fell on it. It was very cooling, and I did not mind. She wiped my face with her handkerchief when we were inside.

My doctor was there. He supervised my transfer to a wheeled table. Two nurses helped the ambulance-men. One of them was elderly and fat; the other was young and pretty and had a brown mole on her chin. I saw the mole even though the hallway was dimly lighted.

A girl who was not a nurse hurried from around the corner of the corridor. She held a sheet of paper in her hand. Bending over it and holding it close to her eyes because of the dim light, she read it to me. It was read hurriedly, some of it, evidently, from memory. Agreement not to hold the hospital responsible for complications.

The girl put the agreement into my hand, leaning it on a thin cardboard, and put a pen in my hand. I began to write, but the cardboard bent back. They lifted me up and I made a cross.

It was painful and I was glad when they let me down and put the ice-bag on again—it had fallen off when I had sat up.

The two nurses wheeled me away, leaving the doctor, Myra and the office-girl looking after me.

In the elevator my feet were pushed up against the iron, grille door; the elevator was narrow. The elevator-man was small and the elevator was of the old "balance" type, so that he had to jump up as far as he could, grab the cable, and let his weight start the lift. We went up very slowly to the top-floor. I knew it was the top, because I saw the gears and wheels through the top of the elevator.

"Careful," the young nurse said to the elevator-man as he was going to jerk open the door. "He's a big man, and his feet are against the door."

"All right, all right," he said, dragging the end of the table sideways out of the way of the door and hurting my big toe as he did it.

He slammed the door open and pulled me out into the corridor.

Everything was quiet. The wheels on my rolling-table had rubber tires, so we made no noise; except the shuffling of the nurses' shoes. We passed a nurse carrying a bed-pan covered with a towel. She did not stop, just went past us quickly.

I turned my head and saw into the open doorways. There were mostly women in the wards. I was beginning to feel like a man who gets into one of those women's tearooms, and who sits, eats, and suffers because he lacks the courage to get up and walk out. I learned later that the men's wards were downstairs.

There was the smell of ether in the air and it became stronger as we went along. We were getting near the operating-room. I was becoming nervous. I had a "wop's" dread of cold steel.

I forgot my nervousness when we were in the anteroom and the nurse took my pajamas off and began to bathe me with warm water. "The old one" shoved my stomach all around. The pain was back and I did not give a damn about anything; only for someone to come and tear it out of me; cut it out; tear it out—anything.

A man came in and watched them for a while. When he saw they were almost done, he went to a long nickeled box and opened it, and a cloud of steam burst out of it. The man—he was dressed in white like the nurses—put on a pair of rubber gloves and took something out of the hot box. He tried to hide it from me, but I saw the large hypodermic needle.

The nurses sat me up.

"Bend over," the man behind me said.

"What for?" I said.

"Never mind, it won't hurt," the man said.

"What're you going to do?"

"Give you spinal anaesthesia. That's what Doctor Herbert said."

"Well, all right," I said.

I bent over, the nurses holding my upper arms. "The old one" was in front of me. There was a coolness, then a stab of pain in the small of my back and the kind of a feeling like when your razor slips and cuts sideways across your face; back and forth slowly several times, my teeth grating on edge. Everything heaved up suddenly and I was sick. I fell forward with my face touching the bare part of the breast of the stout nurse in front, and the smell of perspiration and talcum powder made me feel worse. She pushed me up, cupped her hand over my forehead, and then leaned me far over. I felt better.

"Lie down," she said after a while.

I did, and she threw a sheet over me and went over to the man and the other nurse. I twisted my head back and saw the man take his arm away from around the young nurse's waist. He laughed.

My back was feeling numb and my fingers and toes were tingling. The tingling changed to numbness and I was dead all over. It was a peculiar sensation.

"How do you feel?" the man asked.

"Pretty good."

"I don't mean that."

He took the sheet off and touched me in several places.

"Feel that?" he said.

"No."

"Okey," he said to the young nurse and she went out.

Two men came in through the swinging doors into the operating room. There were two nurses and two men more there, hurrying around, folding towels and pads. They all wore rubber gloves and had masks over their mouths and noses.

The two men ranged themselves alongside me, and one put his arms around my chest; the other, around my hips. A nurse took my legs, and another my head, and they lifted me to the table standing under a glaring, round light. It was like floating, because I could not feel their grips, only the one who took my head. My body was not there at all. I felt only the warm pad under my head.

The man who had administered the needle wrapped a towel around my head. The nurses covered me with towels.

Two men came in through the swinging doors. They were in white and wore masks, and by the stir they all made, I knew the big show was on.

They all lined themselves around me as though they knew their places. The nurse handed the doctor a knife; it glittered in the sharp light.

"I want to see," I said.

"No," the man at my head said.

"Goddamn it, I want to see."

"Lift that head-rest a little and hold a towel in front of his mouth," the surgeon said. His voice sounded far away.

The head-rest was lifted a little and I could see over my chest to my stomach. The towels had been taken off my stomach. My chest still had a towel on it, and so did my legs.

One of the men painted the entire stomach with iodine.

They all stood quite still. The doctor poised. It was like a baseball game, and the batter up at bat. The doctor measured with the knife in the air, made a few fast passes, and swooped, and a mouth began to open on my stomach, fat-bubbles pushing themselves out of the lips. A little trickle of blood ran slowly down and disappeared along the scrotum.

My teeth were chattering and biting against each other. The man at my head looked down at me, saw my face, and quickly and easily lowered the headrest. Something was coming out of me, something from deep down, like a retch does. It rasped my throat and came again and then again. It sounded like a hoarse roar in my ears. I tried to tell the man that it was not my fault; that I was not afraid; that it was not me and was not a part of myself. He looked at me and then at the doctor. Then, he pushed a mask down on my face.

"Breathe!"

I breathed. At first, it was very easy, but then I began to choke. I wanted to throw myself off the table, but I could not. Two fingers were pressed under my jaws and I had to breathe. A buzzing, and a roar, and an automobile horn began to blow loud, and then thin away, going away and then farther but not dying out, like a piece of paper that is cut in half and in half again, and reaching no end because there is always a half left. Then, it reversed and was coming back. Suddenly, it was very funny and I laughed. Everything cleared and I heaved up, only to be held back by the nurse.

I was very sick for a few hours, vomiting bile. Where they had operated, there was no pain.

VII

My room in the hospital was "semi-private," but the other bed was not occupied, and I had the room to myself. Propped up the way I was with pillows, I could see out of the window and over the trees to the street and the elevated-railway. The trains would swing around the curve from in back of the hospital and pull up to the station just in front. The hospital, itself, was very old. If I twisted far over, I could see the wall of the south wing with its red, peeling paint, and dirty, white, wooden sun-porches.

The first day nobody had been permitted to see me, because I ran a temperature. They told me that Myra had been there. The second day, the temperature went down and they let her in.

"Hello," she said.

"Hello."

"How do you feel?"

"So-so," I said.

"They wouldn't let me in yesterday."

"I had a temperature." I felt slightly proud.

"Is it normal?"

"It's normal, now."

I lay back. We did not speak for a while. I kept looking at the crack in the ceiling that ran across the room like the river on a map.

Pretty soon she said: "I phoned Mr. Tinevelli. He's coming over today."

I did not say anything.

"I called the station and told them."

"Thanks," I said. "I forgot about it."

"There was an item about it in the papers."

"I guess 'Hizzoner' will be here. The punk! All dressed up like a house on fire."

"He's your friend."

"The hell he is."

"Don't get excited; it isn't good for you."

"Even thinking about it burns me up."

"You mustn't let it."

"Guess not."

We sat silent again. We were not very talkative; there was not much to say.

The nurse came in—the same one who had the mole on her chin. She was my day-nurse. The mole did not look bad; in fact, it looked attractive. It held your attention to the face, and it was not a bad face.

"A man outside," she said.

"I think I better go," Myra said and got up.

"Who is it? Tell him to come on in."

Teeny came in before the nurse could call him. He passed Myra, who was going out, and nodded to her. She smiled to him and went out. He sat down in the chair she had vacated.

"Why didn't you tell me you were going?" he said.

"Didn't know. It caught me all of a sudden. Anyway, what's it to you?"

"Don't be sore."

"Why shouldn't I be sore?"

"I have enough without that."

"I can't figure you, Teeny. Where'd it go to?"

"Where did what go to?"

"Oh, hell!"

"Buck—if I could tell you, I would, honestly I would."

"So I ain't to be trusted. Christ, I'm in a position to pull you out of any kind of a mess. Why didn't you, why don't you take advantage? I'm willing."

"It's not what's gone before. It's what will happen if I say anything."

"Don't talk riddles," I said.

"I was reading a book review," he said, and he spoke quietly and slowly, "and the fool who was writing—he was discussing a book—said that what the book dealt with went out of date with hooped skirts in the nineteenth century. If they only knew."

"What?"

"Nothing."

"There you go," I said. "What about the kids?"

He jumped up and sat down again and said: "Lay off, Buck. It's them I'm thinking of all the time."

"Did you think about them when you 'tapped'?"

"That's the funny part of it; I did."

"They got it?"

"No, they didn't get it, but it was for them that I did it."

"You giving me the run around?"

"Forget it, Buck."

"Whatever it is, it's dirty, and I can't tie you up with anything crooked. Me, I'm different. I guess we're such friends and stayed friends because we're so different."

"Different, Buck?" He sat looking down at the hat in his lap. "I don't know. You and I are a hell of a lot alike. The only differences are that I am unlike you physically, and that I had parents who were good to me."

"That wouldn't make a difference."

"It did," he said.

"Maybe."

Teeny got up and stood turning his hat in his hands.

"Well—I think I'll go," he said.

"If you want any help, any time, Teeny; you know."

"I suppose sometime there'll be an end. I keep putting it out of my head and trying to stave it off, but it'll have to come to an end sometime. Well, so-long, Buck."

"So-long, Teeny."

He went out. The nurse came over from the other side of the room. She had been sitting on the wide window-sill, reading a book. She smoothed out my pillows.

"Want to lay back?" she asked.

"All right, Miss Hert."

After the head-rest was down, I lay there looking up at her.

"You're pretty," I said.

She smiled. "I've heard that somewheres before," she said.

"Well, you are," I said and reached up and ran the back of my hand along her groin.

"Don't excite yourself. You'll hurt yourself," she said, laughing.

I did not take my hand away.

"The first few days, it's dangerous," she said.

"Later?"

"Perhaps," she said and smiled again.

"Hizzoner," the mayor, arrived with a rush. One minute it was quiet, and the next, everything was in an uproar. He had a crowd of reporters with him and the noise they made with their photographic flashlights and their talk was so much that we could not speak. The smoke from the flashlights made me cough. It hurt, but the nurses and internes were so anxious to get into the pictures that they forgot about me.

One reporter had a new type of "flash": it worked by shooting a blank cartridge, and every time he shot it off, everybody jumped and then laughed.

The mayor was dressed as he always was, like something out of a men's furnishings window. It was only since his election that he dressed that way. He must have learned it from his friend, the Commissioner.

In the end, I was not able to talk with him and he went out as rapidly as he had come in, and everything was quiet again.

Miss Hert opened the windows to let the smoke out. She came over and covered me to the neck with the blanket.

"I could stand a drink," I said.

"I'll get it for you," she said.

"Not water; liquor."

"Do you drink a lot?"

"What do you call a lot?"

"Every day," she said.

"Yes."

"I don't suppose we'll have any trouble with the doctor. I know they prescribe it where a patient is accustomed to liquor."

"Three cheers," I said. "When do we start?"

"I'll go down to the office. We have a supply."

"Make it brandy."

She went and came back in a little while.

"Nothing doing till your doctor comes," she said.

"Hell!"

"You said it. I was all set myself."

"When does he come?"

"About five."

"Guess it'll have to keep till five; but it's a long time—come here and give me a kiss."

"No."

"Come on! I need something to stimulate."

"If you'll promise to be good?"

"Okey!"

She bent over me and I saw the mole coming towards me, and now it was hidden and I felt her lips. She straightened suddenly and slapped my hand away.

"Nix, busyhands," she said.

"Come on."

"Don't be a fool. You're not in condition."

"I am, and how."

"Better use the bed-pan, before you hurt yourself."

"No."

"You'll have to; it's too early yet. Later on, maybe. It'll keep. Here, use the pan. Easy now, don't strain. All right."

"When are they going to take the stitches out?" I asked.

"You haven't any stitches."

"What've I got?"

"Little silver clips. A new thing. They clip into both sides of the cut and hold it together," she said.

"When do they take them out?"

"About three days more."

"Hurt?"

"A little."

"After that, okey?"

"Yes."

They took the little silver clips out on the fifth day. My doctor did it himself. It was not much; just insert a small metal pry and snap up and it was out and without any pain. The pads were put back and the bandages wound around me again.

The doctor went out and Miss Hert and I were left alone. She went over and sat down on the window-sill and opened her book. I knew she was not reading.

"How about it?" I said.

She broke into a smile and said: "How about what?"

"You know."

"I don't know."

"Quit stalling," I said, "and come on."

"Really, I don't know what you mean," she said and got up and came over and stood near the bed. "What do you mean?"

I took her hand and pulled on it, making her sit on the bed. With my arm around her, I said: "I'll show you what I mean," and proceeded to show her what I meant.

We did not say anything for a while, then: "You didn't have to tear the ribbon."

"I'm that way," I said.

"You did it to be smart. I shouldn't let you do anything. You're too smart."

"I didn't do it to be smart—is that your heart?"

"Yes."

"That's funny, I never felt one so strong."

"Never mind my heart—wait a minute, I'll lock the door."

A little later, when I was alone, The Yid came in. I was surprised to see him.

"How come?" I asked.

"I saw it in the city papers, so we came right away."

"We?"

"The wife and me. She's over the room getting washed up. We just got in—if it's all right with you, I ain't here officially. We got to go flat hunting."

"One of the pleasures of married life."

"Aw, cut it. It ain't so bad. Wait'll you see her. You'd do the same."

"I never wanted a woman so bad that I had to marry her to get it," I said.

"This is different. We—what's the use! Let it pass."

A nurse came in and began to straighten things, making a noise when the glass bottles hit against the metal table.

The Yid got up and said: "I'll be back later with the wife," and he went out.

"Where's Miss Hert?" I asked the nurse.

"She's sick; I'm relieving her. I'm the ward-nurse."

"What's the matter with her?"

"She has heart attacks. She's got a leak. The least little strain and she's off."

"Is it bad?"

"She gets it bad."

"I'm going up to see her," I said.

"You can't get off the bed."

"I'm. going up."

"No, you're not!"

We argued and I made a motion to get off the bed without any help; and in the end, they brought in an invalid-chair and sat me in it.

The nurse rolled me down the hall to the elevator and left me with the elevator-man. We went up to the top-floor. He pushed me along to a door, opened it, and pushed me in.

There was a nurse sitting on a trunk near the window. Miss Hert was on the bed.

I looked at her—Jesus Christ, her heart! It was jumping an inch with every beat. I could see the bed cover come up and then fall back, and then, her eyes would roll back. Every time her eyes would roll back, I would grit my teeth. I thought she was dying.

"Do you have to roll your eyes?" I asked.

She did not answer, but rolled her head slowly from side to side.

"I guess it was the excitement," I said. "I'm sorry."

The nurse sitting on the trunk said: "It's your fault."

I became angry and said: "Who're you?"

"She's my friend. We're from the same town. I came down to keep an eye on her."

"I didn't know," I said. "Otherwise . . ."

Miss Hert spoke, and it was more like gasping: "Not your fault. Ever since—husband died—can't stay away from it."

The three of us there in silence, not saying anything, thinking our own thoughts, and the sick-one, maybe, not having any thoughts.

Pretty soon, I said: "Who's going to push me down?"

"I'll push you to the elevator," the nurse on the trunk said and got up.

"I hope you feel better," I said to Miss Hert. She did not answer.

All the rest of the morning and afternoon, I kept thinking about Miss Hert and asking the nurse about her.

The sun was going down. I could see it from my window. The elevated-trains were very numerous. It was the "rush-hour" when people come home. Train after train with rows of lighted windows swung around the curve, stopped, and went on. Watching it, I forgot the nurse. She snapped on the light.

"Put out that light," I said.

"There's somebody here," she said.

I looked up and saw The Yid. He stepped aside a little and said: "Meet the wife—Beth, meet the chief."

She was beautiful!

"Henry's God," she said in a low voice.

I wanted to say something clever. Now that I think of it, I could have said, "Hardly that," but I did not; only, "How are you?"

The nurse put her hand on my forehead. Her hand felt cool.

"Better go," she said. "He has a temperature."

"I hope you feel better," Mrs. Levinson said and smiled and went out with The Yid.

"Put the light out."

"I have to give you an alcohol-sponge."

"Alcohol-sponge be damned! Put out the light."

She snapped out the light. In the dark, I asked: "How's Miss Hert?"

"She's dead. Died about an hour ago."

Quiet; then me: "Son-of-a-bitch!"

I watched the thin strip of light where the sun had gone down. Beth, beautiful, The Yid's wife. . . . And I was suddenly back years; time reduced to nothing. The night is hot and I go out of the stifling tenement and to the roof where most of the neighbors are sleeping and I stop and look long at a woman whose nightdress has rolled up; she is fat and looks like a picture of Venus I once saw in the Museum; filled with looking, I go around the big chimney to lie down on the small space behind it, and someone is there: Nina; the moon shines on her, her feet, her small breasts; she looks like a grey, soap-stone statue; I kneel down and put my arms around her and kiss her breasts; she is frightened, but, my lips against her lips; "Nina, *mia Nina, bella angela*"; whisper, *"Mia bella angela"*—and the moon making shadows on the chimney behind us. And the days go past like that and the roof becomes a shrine, and then she disappears and I go back to the call-houses. I do not see her again, until years later; she is in the line-up when we raid a house; and the little they had left me goes out of me.

I looked, and there was no more light in the sky.

BOOK TWO

VIII

I returned to work without taking any time for rest—and the doctor had told me to rest. With everything that I had on my mind, I could not stop and do nothing. When I tried, faces began to flash before my mind: Stein, "Big Stem," Wallace, Miss Hert; and they would all change and merge and have the face of Beth—and Christ knows, I did not want to think about her.

In the station-house, everybody came up to me and shook hands and asked how I was. I knew it did not matter to them, but I said, "all right," until it became painful and I went up to my office. Captain MacDunn came with me.

I took off my hat and coat.

"Anything new?" I said.

"Not a hell of a lot. I got your share at home."

"Wasn't afraid of that. I know you."

"Thanks—Tom Wallace's been in, and's been calling up. He wants you."

"What for?"

"I ain't supposed to know, but I got an idea."

"What?"

"Phony tickets. Somebody's got out a slew of counterfeit tickets for the fight."

"That's a new wrinkle."

"It's a dandy. You can't tell the good ones from the phonies. There'll be a lot of work for the riot-squad."

"You know anything about him and Stein—Mike Stein?"

"They're pals. Stein gets tickets from Wallace; Stein's 'steerers' send the people across the street—they opened a new branch just in front of the Stadium; got a speakeasy in the back—we get paid to run in the bootleg 'scalpers'; and it's a rosy ring all around."

"Got an idea on the phonies?" I said.

"Lots."

"I guess I got the same idea. Give Wallace a buzz and tell him I'll be there tomorrow, ten o'clock. Tell him to make sure Stein's there too. I got lots to say to both."

"All right."

I got up and picked up my coat and hat.

"Where's The Yid?"

"I put him on beat. No use of him running around loose."

"Put him back on 'special-detail' when he gets back—you don't like him?" I said.

"It ain't that. You got no right to treat a flat-foot like he was an equal."

"I like him; he's good company."

"It ain't right."

"Never did it in front of anybody."

"No, but they know you favor him—and a kike, at that."

"Nix, Mac. What's the difference? He's a good kid. Just got married."

"I know. The whole goddamn station-house knows it," he said.

"You ever love a woman, Mac?"

"No."

"Never?" I asked.

"Never," he said.

"Not even when you're a kid?"

"No."

"Maybe you don't get me. Not when you're old—kids, thinking about nothing but . . ." I was thinking of Nina, and the hot nights, and her nightdress wet with perspiration clinging to my skin.

"I never had it," he said.

"You're a liar."

He walked over to the window and stood there, looking out. Presently, he turned around and said: "When I was a kid—just got over—I fell into a coal-chute."

"Tough," I said. "How old are you?"

"I'm forty-two."

"You look like sixty-two."

"I know," he said; then, with a nod of his head and a wink of his eyes: "Sleeping out, all kinds of weather—Oh, hell! Sometimes a man's a long time getting a break."

"You said it, Mac. Well, so long."

"You ain't going to say nothing?"

"What about?" I said.

"About me and the coal-chute."

"Forgot it already. Let's drink on it."

I went over to the desk and threw my hat and coat on it and opened the drawer, took out three bottles and two glasses.

"Name your poison: Gin, Scotch, or Brandy?"

"Scotch."

"Patriotic, Mac?"

"To hell with that."

I went out and down the street and around a few blocks on the avenue. The new ticket agency was just across from the Stadium. I went into the agency and asked for "Big Stem James." They told me that he was not there but that I might find him in the other agency. I walked through the theatrical district to the agency and went in and spoke to one of the boys behind the counter lined with telephones.

"'Big Stem' around?"

"No, he don't show up mornings. What do you want? Want a pair? I can fix you up."

"No, I don't want any tickets."

"You're Inspector Safiotte?"

"Yes."

"I once got you a 'frame' of seats."

"I don't remember," I said.

"Don't make any difference. I want to speak to you, Inspector, but like man to man," he said.

"What—all right."

"Three years ago, I got a gun-permit from the precinct. Last year, I was out of town and wasn't here to renew it. I made out an application this year. A cop came around, and he don't like the way I was combing my hair, or maybe my signature was written too good—so he rejects me. Now, I got the gun on my hands. I want to get rid of it."

"Where you got it?"

"Uptown."

"Bring it down," I said.

"I'm afraid I'll get picked up," he said.

"Pack it up in some newspaper, like a package. Ask for me. If I'm not there, ask for Mr. Schlegel—he's my civilian clerk. Leave it with him."

"Okey, Inspector. Here's Jamesie's address. You can find him there now; he never gets up before the afternoon. It's room nine thirteen."

I took the address and went out. It was not very far. On the way, I stopped at Monk's newsstand. He came out from behind the counter and shook hands.

"How're you, Looey?" he said, rubbing the handkerchief against his nose and showing me his wide nostrils. "Sniff, sniff. I read the papers."

"All right, Monk."

"I coulda saved you a lot of worry and dough."

"How?"

"Amber beads," he said.

"Amber beads?"

"Yeah. Doctor Wiley—he's dead now—old Jew-doctor, he told my sister. You wouldn't believe it. Neighbor of my sister's; one kid dies in a day—croup; the other one gets sick; my sister's kid gets it; and Doctor Wiley says, a string of amber beads around her neck; and in a shake she's all right. You wouldn't believe it. See, look here," and he pointed to a dark spot on his lip. "Pulled out three hairs, got blood-poison and almost died; a string of amber beads saves me. I coulda loaned you mine."

"Too bad," I said. "You're a good guy anyway."

"I'm a bum."

"You're a good guy."

"Paper; take a paper, Chief?"

"Some other time, Monk," I said and walked away, up the street to the second-rate hotel in which "Big Stem" lived.

I did not stop at the desk, but went through to the elevator. It carried me to the ninth floor.

I knocked on the door several times before there was an answer. "Big Stem", in a pair of dirty pajamas, came to the door and let me in. There was a woman asleep in the bed. He cautioned me to talk low.

"She's tired," he said. "Had almost a line-up last night."

"You pimping, too?"

"Chris', no."

"What she doing here then?"

"Hell—I'm her man. I don't need her dough. Got plenty."

"Since when?"

"Aw, Cap, I'm all right, now."

"You get what I wanted?"

"Sure," he said and went to the dresser and took a card out of the drawer. "Here it is."

"How'd you get it?"

"Tailed her."

The woman on the bed opened her eyes and said: "Some day, you goin' to get rubbed out for that big yap of yours."

"Aw, honey, Mame, darling, I ain't tellin' him anything everybody don't know."

"All right, wise-guy, always tryin' to show how much you know; how many big-shots you have business relations with. One of these fine days there ain't gonna be no more 'Big Stem.'"

"The Cap and me is old friends, Mame," he said and looked around the room. "Ain't what it used to be, eh, Cap?"

The woman became angry: "You can't forget it?"

"No, I can't," he said. "And lemme tell you something: if I'm this way next year, it's the pipe for me."

"Aw, nuts, why wait?"

While they were quarreling, I turned the card over and looked at it; it was a picture of a boy of about five years. James saw me looking at it.

"Some boy!" he said.

"Nice feller," I said.

"My boy—you don't have to say it; don't I know it. Sure, I should be ashamed—got a nice mother. Pay her fifteen a week alimony. Ain't I a goddam bum? Look at him. Ain't I a goddam bum? You didn't know about it, did you?"

"Horse manure," the woman on the bed said.

The next morning, The Yid and I were in the corridors of the Stadium at ten o'clock. We stopped and looked at some of the pictures that lined the walls. They were all the same; the same facial expressions; the same flat noses and smashed ears; and the same effort of the photographer to make a "pug" look like a Greek athlete. Someone—I guess the same mind which thought of fixing referees—had got the idea of decorating the walls. The last time I had been there, it was plain concrete and cement and in keeping with the purpose; now, it was decorated like a dance-hall. Walls painted to look like marble only look like walls painted to look like marble.

A man was coming down the corridor; he was tall and walked with so much of a limp that he needed the support of a cane. I knew his face but did not know where I had seen him. When I stopped him and asked the way to Wallace's office, he said: "Who sent you this way?"

"The special cop on the door," I said.

"He's not a regular; he's with the show here now, so he wouldn't know. You go outside and around the corner to the executive offices."

I said, "Thank you," and his face creased with a friendly smile. I smiled back at him.

The elevator man, after taking us up, pointed out the office to us. We went in. There was a very fat girl sitting at a typewriter. I told her who I was and she went through a door marked "private," came out and told us to wait a few minutes.

I said in a whisper to The Yid: "How would you like to meet that in the dark when it's in heat?"

He said something in Yiddish.

"What does it mean?" I asked.

"God forbid."

"Say it again."

He said it and I repeated it after him.

I walked around the room looking at the trophies and the pictures. I came to one picture, and I knew then who the man with the limp was—whatever else Wallace was, he never forgot a friend—it was the man who had staked him out west.

A buzzer sounded and the girl told me to go in. I opened the door myself and went in. Wallace was sitting in front of the desk, Stein on it, and another man, whom I knew immediately, was standing near Wallace, reading a letter in an undertone, mumbling the words to himself.

"That's fine," he said and gave the letter to Wallace who signed it.

Stein got off the desk. He was small and sleek and had shiny black hair which he wore straight back and brushed flat.

"Inspector, meet Mr. Reincad," he said.

"I know Mr. Reincad," I said. "He once broke ground for a school in a precinct of mine."

"Which one?" Reincad said. He talked through his nose and the fat pouches on his face quivered when he spoke.

"Union and Center."

"Yeah, I built that."

"Sit down, Inspector," Wallace said.

I sat down.

"Mr. Reincad is arranging a benefit. Here you are, Reincad," he said and handed him the letter.

Reincad picked it up and looked at it again.

"Fine," he said and put the letter into his pocket, put on his hat and coat, said good-bye, and went out.

"That's a hot one!" Stein said. "That guy can't read or write, only sign his name. He wouldn't let on he can't, so he mumbles it to himself."

"More power to him," I said. I was ready to quarrel about anything with Stein.

"Right, Safiotte," Wallace said. "More power to him. Comes here from Russia in the steerage; sells newspapers; picks his meals out of the garbage cans—told me that himself—now, the Soviet Government offers him a hundred and ninety million dollar job, forty years of work."

"They'll never pay it," Stein said.

"He's not dumb enough to take it," Wallace said. "Why did you want Stein here, Safiotte?"

"He'd been here anyway, and I wanted to show you I was wise."

"Wise to what?"

"Anything you say. You tell me."

"What are you driving at?" Stein said.

"Me? I'm driving at nothing, only getting in ahead of you," I said. "Tell the sad story."

"I asked you to come here as an officer of the law," Wallace said.

"No? Go on."

"We're in a pickle. Somebody's let loose a load of counterfeit tickets. There's going to be hell to pay."

"Where'd they come from?"

"Most of them came from the 'scalpers.'"

"Where'd they get 'em?" I asked.

"They say they got them from the box-office. They would—the damn liars."

"What do you want me to do?"

"We want what we're entitled to," Stein said.

"Protection against fraud."

"Why don't you ask your friend downtown?"

"Don't have to."

"Listen, Stein," I said. "We ran together a long, time, you and me and Tim. Lately, you two ain't been so friendly, and I don't see you much. Because I don't run with you anymore don't mean I've gone all of a sudden dumb. I can see when somebody wants to give me a push and lead me along a steer so I don't see the other."

"What the hell do you mean?" Stein shouted. He was very angry and looked like a jay-bird hopping around.

"You know," I said.

"Wait a minute," Wallace said quietly. He always spoke softly. "Will you explain, Inspector?"

"I'm willing to ride along if you come across," I said. "You know those tickets came out of the box-office. Only known scalpers were fed them. Whoever thought of that one—and I got an idea who did—it's a beaut; you get rid of competition and you make a quarter of million for yourself, less what you have to pay the box-office for their split. Stein, I don't see why I don't take my hat off and stand in respect to you."

He smiled, then looked at Wallace, and Wallace nodded and said: "If we ring you in—and mind you, I'm not saying anything—what then?"

"Is there any way of telling the phonies from the good ones?"

"The key on the seal is twisted on the phonies."

"All right," I said. "First, we clean the scalpers."

"Don't hold them," Wallace said.

"I know," I said. "The riot—and the bomb-squads will do the rest the night of the fight."

"You're in," Wallace said.

"How about the papers?" I asked.

"The boys will find the usual envelope in the box-office. They'll be all right," he said.

"What's my split?" I asked.

"Ten percent," Stein said.

"Of what?"

"You'll have to trust us."

I laughed and said: "I'll leave it to Wallace, not to you."

We shook hands all around. I picked up my hat and said: "Stein, I want to see you private."

"All right," he said and followed me.

I turned around when I got to the door and said to Wallace: "How come all the wise-money is on Tierney?"

"He's in better condition than he was last year," Wallace said.

I looked at him hard and said, "Maybe," and went out, Stein following me.

In the hall, he said: "What do you want, Buck?"

I said: "Wait a minute. Yid, walk down the hall a ways."

The Yid walked away.

"You still good friends with Tim?"

"Yes."

"He's going to have a chance to prove what kind of a good friend he is."

"How come?"

"Three reasons: number one, counterfeit tickets; number two, referee fixing; number three, Rose Moore."

When I said the name, he became white and leaned up against the wall. "You double-crossing bastard," he said.

"Only you, nobody else, Stein."

"What do you want?"

"You know what I want. All you got to do is see Tim. Hell of a note for a mayor to be running with you. It would look nice in the papers, Children's Society and all. He'll come across just to keep himself out of it,"

I left him standing in the hall.

IX

I counted time from its distance to the big-fight; and it was just three weeks before the fight that Teeny came. It was morning, and in the strong sunlight that came in through the window, I could see the nervous twitching of his face muscles. He looked around to see if anybody was there with me; I was alone—The Yid was always coming late since he had been married.

"Sit down, Teeny, and take it easy," I said.

He sat down, put his elbow on the desk and rested the side of his head on his hand.

"Finished," he said.

"Come to a head?"

"Yes. I got a tip-off: bank examiner is coming in next week."

"Let's have it, Teeny!"

"Jesus Christ!" and he began to cry.

I did not say anything, and let him cry. Some men are like that. Me, I became dried up long before I knew what tears were for. Pretty soon, he stopped crying. His eyelashes were wet and his face was streaked.

"I suppose I should start and say the same old thing: 'What a fool I've been'?" he said. "I have no excuse for myself——if I told you my excuse, you'd think I was crazy."

"Tell it," I said.

"I love my wife—you must get that straight first. She's been a damn good wife and mother, and I love her."

He looked at me and then out of the window and continued: "You can love a woman and not be satisfied; and that's my excuse."

Again there was a long silence. Then: "They laid for me with a girl. Beautiful—Buck, she was as beautiful as only a woman made for dirt can be. I got drunk, dirty, filthy, lousy drunk, and didn't remember anything till I got up in the hotel; she was still there next to me. That day, somebody came and showed me a picture." The tears started to run down his face. "I nearly threw up; I couldn't believe it was me; I couldn't believe I could do it; but it was me all right. It was a frame." Pause again. "I made out a set of notes and I've been paying ever since. One's due tomorrow."

"Who are they?" I asked.

"I can't tell you. I never saw the girl again after that day. Who's behind it, I don't know; I deal through a go-between."

"Who's he?"

"I can't tell you, Buck."

"Why?"

"Something worse will happen."

"You can't be worse off; and if I nab them, I'll make sure they won't be able to talk."

"That won't stop it."

"How d'you expect me to help you if you don't come across?"

"All I want is for you to send a man out to the house and keep him there day and night."

"They threaten that?"

"No, but they're capable. I'm going to protest the note. It'll be less to pay the bank in the end. I should've done it in the first place, but—you know how it is—afraid to face it." Pause. "The kids, Jesus Christ, the kids!"

"How about yourself?"

"They wouldn't hurt me. I'm too much of a meal ticket."

"All right. I'll send a man out tomorrow. It's out of my district, but I'll send somebody we can trust. The Yid—know him? Instead of two men in shifts, you better have him sleep there and eat there."

"I'll try to arrange it without scaring the Misses."

"When you protesting the note?"

"Tomorrow."

"If you need money?"

"No."

"The Yid" came in, and he looked tired; there were circles under his eyes.

"Don't agree with you?" I said.

"Too much," he said and laughed.

"You're going to get a rest."

"How come?"

"You know Tinevelli's place on The Island?"

"Yep."

"Go out there tomorrow and stay there. Keep your eye on the Misses and the kids, especially at night. Keep your gun handy."

"Hell—and me just married."

"Can no help, Yid. Take the day off and fill up. Be out there in the morning and don't leave till you get told from me. I'll bring your wife out a couple of times so you won't burn up."

Four days passed. I had been busy clearing the speculators who had the counterfeit tickets. They were not told that the tickets were wrong. We would take them in and take the tickets away from them and bring them up before the judge in the usual way. If the tickets were good, I would turn them back to Wallace and he would resell them; if they were bad, I would destroy them. I kept several counterfeits; I had no doubt that it would not be difficult to trace them to the printer.

The Yid called me by telephone during the morning of the fifth day that he was away. His voice sounded angry.

"He ain't showed up all night," he said.

"Who?"

"Tinevelli. I don't give a damn; I wasn't told to nurse-maid him, but the old lady's driving me nuts."

"Did you call the bank?"

"Yes. No answer."

"Sure she was ringing the right number: they're dumb."

"Sure. Called a couple of times. The last time she told me the service was temporarily disconnected," he said.

"Tell the Misses I'll get hold of him; he maybe stayed in the city and forgot to phone."

"I thought you was going to bring the wife?"

"So that's what's eating you!"

"It ain't eating me."

I put my cheek against the transmitter and looked across the desk at the wall.

"Hello—you there?" he said, thinking we had been disconnected.

"Be out today, if I find him or no," I said.

"How about the wife?"

"She'll be there."

"Outside that, this is a cinch: swell feed, swell room I got—say, why can't the wife stay here, too?"

"You're on duty, that's why. Maybe if I sent you but on a night assignment, you'd want your bed and wife along. It wouldn't hurt you to lay off; you look like you been sleeping on your face continuous for a year."

"When I get as old as you . . ."

"Don't get gay. I can go you time for time."

"I don't mean that. I know you could. Aw, hell—I love her."

I laughed into the telephone.

"You go to hell!" he said.

"After I bring your darling or before?"

"After."

"I'll be out—maybe she wouldn't be home?"

"She'll be home."

"God! What a trust!" I said.

"Don't start any of that," he said.

"Calm yourself, lovebird."

"You think I'd let her go with you if I didn't know her? I wouldn't trust you with a rubber doll."

"Now you're getting sloppy. Don't get sloppy," I said.

"How about hanging up?"

"Good idea."

"You bringing the wife?"

"Yes, for Chrissake, yes!"

I let him hang up and pushed the receiver hook down several times to call the operator. When she answered, I gave her the bank's number. After a few seconds, another voice said that the service had been temporarily disconnected.

"This is the Police Department," I said.

"Just a moment, I'll give you the manager."

The manager told me that he was sorry, but the connection had been discontinued at the request of the subscriber, and he could not do anything. I said, "thank you," and hung up.

It was noon before I could get away to go downtown.

Outside, it was warm for that time of the year. The sun was shining and it was amusing to see how most of the people walked on the side of the street which the sun shone on and how leisurely they walked, and how the few who walked on the shady side hurried along.

I did not keep my car in the police garage, but in a private garage a few blocks away. Walking along in the direction of the garage, I thought of The Yid's wife; I wanted to think of Teeny, but I could not—only she kept coming.

I drove the car out of the garage and moved slowly along in the heavy traffic; because of the nice weather, there were more cars than usual. Whenever I was out in front, the plates on my car would keep me from being held at the crossings, but when there were cars in front of me I had to wait. Towards the East Side, the traffic became clearer and I went faster, and on the avenue running downtown, I put on a burst of speed that brought me into Little Italy in a short time.

There was a group of people in front of the bank. The door was closed, and a sign was hanging on it. One man was reading in a low voice to the others; they were clustered around him. One, a little man with a large mustache that covered half his face, made a bitter remark in Italian. A woman ran up to them and began to curse, showing a knowledge of abnormal sex relations that only an Italian slut could possess. She stuck her tongue out and moved her hands and fingers suggestively, accompanying her motions with direct accusations against the morals of Teeny, his wife, his parents, and those even remotely connected with him.

I got out of the car and pushed my way through to the door. One of them must have recognized me, because they stopped talking loudly, whispered a little, and were quiet.

I read the notice; it was notifying the depositors that the bank examiners were closing the bank for a complete check up.

When I rapped on the door with my large signet ring, nobody came. I kept rapping until a man came to the door. He was very angry and, from behind the glass, made motions for me to go away. I showed him my badge, and he went back and came back with another man who had the key in his hand. They let me in, slamming the door behind me as though a mob was rushing up to get in. I looked back; the crowd outside had not moved.

"Is Mr. Tinevelli here?" I said.

The man who had come last, looked at me hard and said: "He certainly is not."

"Know where I could find him?"

"Can you tell us? We'd like to know."

"What's the matter?" I said.

"Are you Captain of this precinct?" He said.

"I'm Inspector Safiotte."

"Well—it's all right to tell you."

"Tell me what?"

"We have a warrant for Tinevelli," he said.

"What for?"

"Larceny."

"How many know it?"

"We two and the judge."

"What judge?"

"Campiglia."

"He's all right," I said. "Can we talk business—Tinevelli's my friend."

"I'm afraid it's too late for that."

"Why?"

"It isn't the short accounts; his personal notes would be all right if he put up his property as security."

"What's the warrant for, then?" I asked.

"False certifications; cheques, certified cheques. They were released a few days ago in a dozen small cities around here, and there were no such accounts here. Tinevelli, himself, certified them; his signature is on them."

"How about the indorsements?"

"Fake! Some of the cheques were in payment of merchandise. The Anita Mills gave two men thirty thousand dollars worth of silk hose on a certified cheque. Who wouldn't? I guess it's grand larceny you're bucking, Mr. Safiotte."

"If you find him, will you call me at the forty-first precinct station before he's booked?"

"I suppose I can do that."

"Thanks," I said.

We shook hands and walked to the door; he opened it and let me out.

The crowd was still there and opened up a path to let me through. The man with the big mustache followed me to the car and asked me in Italian if they were going to lose their money. They were poor people, he said. Could not the police do something about getting their money? There were five children at home and he had already made another which was yet in its mother's belly. Could not the police do something about the money? He had sweated blood (Italians do not sweat perspiration, only blood) to get together the few dollars. Big tears began to roll down his face and into his mustache, and his nose began to run, too. He wiped his nose with his sleeve, saying that he would have justice. He had his first papers and was entitled to justice. The others, foreigners, he said with a wave of his hand; they were not entitled to justice. He was a citizen. He would demand that the police get him his money back.

I told him to shut up; that everything was all right. He smiled, his nose still running, turned around and ran over to the crowd and talked rapidly.

I drove away.

X

It was late afternoon when I drove up to the house in which The Yid lived. I got out of the car on the far side because there was a baby-carriage in the way on the pavement side.

The house was like all the other far uptown apartments. It was built with the idea of crowding all the apartments possible into the available space. The entrance was an alley which looked as though it had been cut into the middle of the house after it had been built. I went down it and it was so narrow that the dim light of the late afternoon did not penetrate into it, and I had to light a match in order to see the names over the bells. I pressed the one marked Levinson and waited a few seconds and there was a buzz which opened the lock on the door. I held the door open and lit another match. The apartment number was seventeen.

I went upstairs, and she was standing in the doorway of the apartment.

"Hello," I said.

"Hello, Inspector. Come in."

I went in and stood in the narrow hallway—everything was narrow here.

"I'm going out to see Henry," I said. "I spoke to him by phone, and he wants me to bring you over."

"Now?" she said.

"Now."

"But I'm not dressed."

I looked at her and smiled and said: "You got clothes on."

"But I'm not dressed for going out."

"Nobody'll see you."

"Isn't there anybody out there?"

"Only the Misses and the kids."

"I'll dress anyway. It'll only take me a few minutes."

"Go ahead," I said. "It's all right."

"Come in and sit down."

I followed her into the parlor; and it was not bad. I knew that The Yid had not had much to say about fixing it up. It was nice.

"I have one," I said, pointing to the baby-grand piano.

"You play?"

"No. When I have—well, company."

"I play a little," she said. "Sit down."

I sat down on the sofa, and she went into the bedroom and shut the door.

Opposite me, hanging on the wall and over a table, was a large picture. I got up and went over to it so that I could see it better; the colors had attracted me. It was a woman and a man in a background of marble; the woman was in black and the man in red; and he had hold of her hand and must have been telling her plenty, because she had a far-away look in her eyes.

All at once it was over me; that was what I had been fighting off. Well, all right. There were some things that would be and you could not blame a man for. So I let myself think and my mind was in the bedroom with her. I was like a virgin boy who waits in the ante-room for his turn and is both afraid and excited.

She came out, dressed for the street, and I decided she was not beautiful but lovely (that was the word)—like a madonna. She was more like the Mother Mary than any woman I had seen. Well, I thought, nothing strange in that: God chose a Jew-girl to have his love affair with. (Funny—thinking of the Mother of God and adultery at the same time.)

"I'm ready," she said.

"Nice apartment," I said.

"I fixed it for comfort. I want it to be like a home."

"I guess it's comfortable."

"Yes. Some people furnish homes for visitors; I want one for my own pleasure."

We went out, and she locked the door.

It was dark when we came out on the street and got into the car. When I shifted the gears to start the car, I touched her leg; I apologized, and she said it was all right.

Riding along, I said: "How do you like the Big City?"

She thought a moment and said: "It's like a prison in which you feel a strange freedom."

What the hell, I thought.

"How can it be both at one time?" I said.

"The houses are like prisons: hundreds of people one over the other; streets without trees . . ."

"What's the freedom if it's like that?"

"Freedom from observation; nobody prying into your affairs. In a small town, you have to be careful of everything you do; in a minute, the telephones are busy telling the world. What you wear is even of interest. If you keep your shades down, you're hiding terrible things. Here—nobody knows you. Even if you did terrible things, nobody would know or care."

"Yes," I said, thinking of the women I had seen, sitting near their baby-carriages in front of the house.

We did not speak for a while. Then, I said: "Did you ever want to do anything terrible?"

"That all depends on what your opinion of terrible is."

"Nothing is terrible to me," I said.

"Some things are."

"No, nothing is. What we do, well, we do because it's in us—you know what I mean."

"Inherent?"

"I don't know," I said.

"Born with you?"

"That's it—'born with you,'" I said. "I can't stop myself from doing some things."

"Then you're putting your appetite, your stomach, where your head should be. Your mind should control your body."

"That's right. My mind thinks and my body follows it up."

"Then you don't think right."

"I'm not responsible for what I think; everything around was made to get it excited."

"You know better."

I caught myself up; I had been talking in the wrong way. "I know better," I said.

Out of the city and on the smooth road, we did not talk. I like driving at night. There is something about the smooth road coming towards you all the time and never ending; you cannot see anything else, only maybe, a fringe of bush and trees. I drove very fast, slowing up for towns.

I swung up the driveway of Teeny's house. The entrance light was on and lighted the red slate slabs on the floor of the open terrace in front of the house.

The door opened, and The Yid ran down the steps.

"I thought you was never coming," he said.

I did not answer him, but while I went up the steps, I heard his wife explaining.

Taking my hat and coat off, I threw them on the big black arm chair—there were two of them, both carved all over with patterns and figures.

The Yid and his wife came in, and the grandfather clock began to chime.

"How lovely," she said.

"Yeah, it's nice," The Yid said.

"Did he show up?" I asked.

"No."

"Phone?"

"No."

The Yid was very snappy, and he kept looking at everything except his wife.

"Where's the Misses?" I said.

"In the kitchen."

"I'll go and talk to her, and you can go upstairs and talk to your wife. I can see you're burning up for conversation."

I thought I heard The Yid say something under his breath; his wife became red.

As soon as Mrs. Tinevelli saw me, she started to cry and the fat all over her shook when she cried; her triple chins, her big breasts and bulging belly quivered. I let her cry and, as soon as she stopped shaking so much, said in Italian: "You know about the bank?"

"Yes," she said. "My friends called up to sympathize and told me—O my Matthew!"

I saw that she was going to erupt again.

"He's all right; keep quiet."

"You know where he is: you saw him?" she said, speaking very rapidly.

"No, I do not know where he is, but he is all right. When this is straightened out, he will come back. Matthew is timid. I am his friend and will do much for him."

She grabbed my arm and began to thank me. Her fingers were like jelly; they were puffed and big with fat and square at the ends.

"Where's Carlo and Mary?" I said.

"In the cellar."

I left her in the kitchen and went down into the cellar. Teeny had fixed up a pool-room there.

The two children, when they saw me on the steps, ran over to me. They were very affectionate and wet my cheek with a kiss each. I laughed. They were not much worried about their father; their own lives occupied them. This, I felt, was true spirit.

The boy—he was ten years old—played several games of pool with me, and the girl stood off and looked on for a short while, then went back to the radio in the corner of the room.

While we were playing, I said to the boy: "When did you see your father?"

"Yesterday morning. It was funny; he kissed me and he was crying. What was he crying about?"

"I don't think he was crying."

We talked while we played, and the radio in the corner kept playing music, with announcements breaking up the music once in a while. How was he getting on at school? He was in the rapid-advance class and was doing a year's work in a half year, he said, and would be getting out soon. Would he go to high-school? Yes, he would, and to college. Did I carry a gun? Yes, I did. Where? It was under my arm. Yes, he could see it.

I took out the gun and he looked at it. Mary came over and stood near us, looking with her dark eyes at the gun. Did I carry it always? Yes, I carried it always. I put the gun back into the arm-holster. The boy sighed and picked up his cue.

Who was Mr. Levinson, he asked. I told him that he was a policeman and was there for their protection and that they were not to go out after dark. Did he, too, carry a gun? He did. Did I think he would let him shoot it if he asked? I said, no; he had to account for every cartridge, but I would come out some day with a boxful of cartridges, and we would shoot. When would I come? Soon, I said.

"Is the key there yet?" I said.

"Yes," he said and put down his cue.

We went through the side door built in the partition which separated the pool-room from the rest of the cellar. In the cellar, the furnace was hot and, with its wide pipes going in all directions, was like a giant octopus. I had to stoop to pass under the pipes.

Carlo went into the dark corner, switched on a light, and took a key off a hook and opened a wooden bin which was there. We went into the big, cool bin. There were several barrels and cases there. He knew which one I wanted and handed me a gallon measure, and I put it under the spigot of one of the barrels and opened it, and the wine, red and dark, gurgled out; it was sour and cool and strong.

While I drank, Carlo said nothing. Finished, I handed him the measure and he put it on the shelf, and after locking the bin we went back into the poolroom. He wanted to play, but I said that I had to go and kissed them and went upstairs.

Mrs. Tinevelli was in the kitchen and I had to go through the same reassurance process.

I sat down in one of the carved chairs in the hall. I was satisfied to wait because the wine had made me a little sleepy.

The clock began to chime, and The Yid and his wife came down the stairs. He was walking a few steps in advance. All his bad humor had melted away. His wife did not look at me and seemed ashamed. She did not say again that the chimes were nice, and I do not think she noticed them.

The Yid wanted to talk, but I said that I did not have any time and that he was to stay until I told him to come back. He said, okey.

All the time that I was getting my coat, putting it on, saying good-bye, and going down the steps, Mrs. Levinson did not look at me.

We started home. She kept her head straight, looking at the road ahead. For a long distance I did not say anything, then: "Yes, I guess it's that way."

She gave a quick look into her lap and then looked ahead again.

It was beginning to rain. First it came in a drizzle and then in a steady downpour that beat itself on the top of the car and against the windows and ran down in little streams on the glass. I put on the windshield-wiper and the swish of it made you think of a rocking chair and the quiet that came of rocking in one.

I spoke again: "Didn't you know it was like that?"

"No."

"Well, it is."

"It doesn't have to be."

"It's always like that."

"He had no right to shame me."

"You're married," I said.

"Yes—we're married," she said.

We rode along a little way in silence.

"Why?" I said.

"Why?"

"Why'd you marry him?"

She did not want to say anything. I slowed down and pulled up on the side of the road and stopped the car, but kept the motor running and the wiper going. I do not know why, but I wanted the wiper going.

"You can talk to me," I said.

She hesitated, then: "It's so hard, but I want to talk, I do so want to talk. I was alone, and he was good to me. I lived with my aunt and uncle."

"No people?"

"No. Father was a tubercular; my mother died watching him. We'd be afraid all day and all night; afraid that he'd start to bleed. The times it happened were terrible—I hate the color red. We'd put a pail in front of him and pack him with ice and run for the doctor. Mother died and left me with it. Once the ice didn't help and he got whiter and redder and bled to—oh, dead—bled to death before the doctor could come."

"Too bad," I said.

"No. I was glad. You don't know how it felt not to be afraid any more. Waiting for the terrible to happen is more terrible than the thing that happens. I went to live with my aunt."

"No good? They were no good?"

"They were too good. They never said anything, but I, myself, felt all the time that I was an outsider and that I was getting charity. I tried to get something, but in a small town it's hard. And then the life: every minute drags. If you want excitement, you have to go out riding with the boys to the woods. There is nothing else to do. Then you marry one of them, and all the rest tell him how good you are—I couldn't stay and do that!"

"Why didn't you leave and come here?"

"You don't know."

"Why?" I said.

"It's hard for a girl, particularly a Jewess. We're orthodox."

"Nobody'd hurt you if you didn't want to be hurt."

"I didn't mean that. I meant how they would feel—when he came on his vacation and was so good, I thought . . ."

"You thought you loved him," I said. "And how about now?"

"I don't know. Gratitude . . . love . . . I don't know."

"I'd never treat the woman I loved like he treated you," I said.

"I don't think you would. Who is she?"

"I never loved anybody. No woman wanted to look at me twice," I said.

"Did you ever give a woman a chance?"

"Not anybody at all. I waited for a good woman," I lied. "And I'm starved for it. I want to love somebody. I could even make love to you."

"Even me?"

I thought she meant it was all right. I put my arms around her and pulled her towards me and said: "Kiss me! Give me a kiss!"

She pushed me. "You're crazy," she said.

"Give me a kiss!"

"You're crazy now. You'll laugh at yourself tomorrow."

I kept pulling her towards me; I wanted to hide my twitching face. I had been smiling, and now, not wanting to smile and wanting to keep my face muscles as though they were, the muscles quivered. I felt like the fool who, laughing at his own joke, suddenly finds nobody laughing with him. She gave me a big push.

My head on my arms on the wheel; I am thinking fast: she has something on you and might tell her husband.

I looked at her, my face serious. "I'm sorry," I said. "I must be crazy, but I'm starved for it."

"It's all right," she said.

"Wouldn't you kiss me?" I said, and when she looked at me, frightened, "not like I wanted—like a brother?"

She looked at my eyes, coming close to see better in the dim light of the dashboard-light, and bent over and kissed me. Her lips were very soft and moist.

"Friends?" she said.

"Friends."

XI

The next day was without an end, but looking at last from the end, it was as though it had never been.

I could not do anything about finding Teeny, because Headquarters was making the usual search for a wanted man. I had called in Captain Mac and told him that if Teeny was picked up in our district he was to keep it quiet.

I was glad it was out of my hands. We were friends, but the way I felt, any kind of activity would not have appealed to me. A desire to sit and do nothing and only think had come over me. To sit and to think; and I saw it before me. Me, standing in the hallway, putting her coat away, and while I would be doing it, she would be pushing her fingers into the bottom of her hair like all women do when they take a hat off. And after I had hung the coat away, I would put my hand under her arm, far under her arm, so that my knuckles would push up against the part where the breast begins and we would go into the parlor. I would bring a drink to warm us inside and to put a little fuel to the burning already there, and maybe it would become too warm and a few clothes would be taken off and we would be there on the couch together. I would love her and play with her, and sometimes she would suddenly put her arms around me, and then just as suddenly lie back again and receive. It would be that way all night; wanting and satisfying, and thinking of nothing, only feeling warm and excited and then quiet.

I was becoming excited thinking about it. It was not like the other times; something that I wanted to get out of me and rid of; but like a feeling between sleeping and waking and nice dreaming.

All day it was like that, and in the end, I decided. To hell with it! Take a chance. It was better than sitting there and dreaming about it.

While I was driving uptown, I thought about The Yid's end of it. It would not be taking anything from him, because he would not know. After a while, it would get cold and hard like the others and it would not matter whom I stayed with.

This time, I did not park in front of the house, but around the corner. I walked quickly to the house, because it was raining. Knowing where the bell was, I did not have to light a match. I pressed the bell and the buzzer sounded and I went in and up, expecting to see her at the door; she was not there. I rang the door bell and heard her coming towards the door.

"Who's there?" she said.

"Inspector Safiotte."

She did not speak for about thirty seconds, then: "Just a minute."

I heard her go back down the hall and come back. She opened the door.

"Hello," I said.

"Good evening."

She was dressed in a kimono. She must have just got up from sleeping—I thought then—because she did not have any cosmetics on. I thought that she was not as pretty without them.

"Like to take a ride?"

"I don't think so."

"Why shouldn't you?"

"Would it be all right?"

"Sure."

"It's raining."

"That's nothing. It's nice in the rain."

Color was coming back into her face, and I knew she had been frightened, and I thought that I had better go slowly.

"All right," she said. "I'll slip a dress on."

She went into the bedroom, came back dressed and went to the closet and put her hat and coat on. She smiled at me and walked down the dark hallway to the door. I followed her. When she put out her hand to open it, I put both my arms around her from behind and pulled her against me. She stood a moment, then all at once, like a woman who faints, went limp against me—so she had been thinking about that kiss, too. It did not feel like anything with two heavy coats between us. I turned her around and began to kiss her, each time harder and the last time so hard that her mouth opened and I kissed her teeth. My lips were moist with the wet from her mouth.

I pulled her towards the parlor.

"No," she said.

"Please," I said. "A few minutes."

"No."

"I love you," I said. I was beginning to believe it myself.

She took her hat off, and I helped her take her coat off; she was acting as though she was very tired. While I removed my coat, she sat on the couch and, with her head turned sideways, looked at the wall.

I sat down, put my arms around her and said: "I love you," and kissed her, and she said, "Buck, Buck."

We were on the couch and I loved her. There was a bird of paradise in bright colors on the mohair of the couch, and while I loved her, she traced the outline of it over and over again with the tip of her index finger, pausing with the finger pointed when I loved her hard.

"Please, Buck, don't. Please, take your hand away."

"I love you," I said. "Don't you love me? Don't you want to belong to me?"

"Yes—don't, Buck, please!"

"Don't you want to belong to me—all of you? I love you. I want all of you."

"You mustn't."

"You're nice, you're beautiful."

She was standing up and crying softly, the tears running down her face, and with her hands brushing out the wrinkles in her dress. The rain made a sharp noise against the window.

I got up and put my arms around her and sat down again with her. I felt warm inside and wanted my arms around her and to feel her against me.

"I feel like a prostitute," she said.

"Don't be foolish. I'm crazy about you, and you're over me—no?"

"Yes."

"Then it's all right. Isn't it all right?"

"Yes," she said.

"Then stop crying."

She wiped her eyes with her handkerchief. Her eyes and nose were red.

I picked her up, and she closed her eyes and shook her head. I said, "Please," and walked towards the bedroom.

"Not in the bed, Buck. It wouldn't be right."

After the rain stopped, it got very cold. Being very late, the steam-heat was shut off, and it was cold in the house.

"I better get a blanket," I said, and I spoke very low.

"You'd better go home; it's very late."

"No."

"Yes. Go home."

"I'm going to stay all night."

"Please, Buck. Let me get used to it. Don't make me feel bad again."

"You shouldn't feel bad," I said and thought, how many times will I have to put up the same damned argument?

"You can't stay here," she said.

"No? Why not?"

"Because—don't you understand?"

"You ever going to spend the night?"

"Maybe; not now."

"When? I want to know."

"Give me a chance."

"I love you," I said, and put my arms around her.

"I know," she said, and she said it as if she was tired of hearing it.

"All right, I'll go home."

She smiled and said: "Now, say it to me," and I said: "You're beautiful, and I love you."

We walked to the door very quietly so that nobody in the next apartment would hear us. At the door, she put her arms around me, and I pushed her against the door and pressed her body hard with mine and kissed her. The metal door was cold against the backs of my hands.

The kimono fell off her shoulders and she was left with her shoulders and part of her breast bare. It excited me and I wanted to turn back, but she pushed me away and opened the door.

"Tomorrow," I said.

"Not here," she answered.

"Where?"

"I don't know."

"I'll write down the address—one o'clock."

"Hurry up, Buck. Somebody might see."

I took my pencil out, tore a piece of paper out of the small note-book which I carried in my pocket, and wrote the address and gave it to her. She took it and began closing the door.

"A good-night," I said.

She put her head around the edge of the door; I held her head and kissed her hard. I knew I was hurting her.

The rain had stopped, but the pavements were still wet and shiny and in some places starting to freeze over. The street lights were reflected in the water and ice, and icicles hung on the metal shields of the lights. It was so cold that I was afraid that the water in the car would be frozen; I remembered that I had no freeze-mixture in it.

The car was standing all wet and shiny where I had left it under a light. The motor did not start, only gave a cough when I got in and pressed the starter and pulled the choke. After pressing the starter several times, the motor caught on. I raced it to warm it up and it backfired a few times because of the open choke.

A man came to the basement-floor window and looked out. Finally, the motor was warm; I shifted the gears and drove away, racing the motor. I did that as a parting shot at the man in the window.

XII

The playing of a radio in the apartment near mine woke me the next morning. I lay in bed, wondering: how people can get up early in the morning, tired and sleepy and with a bad taste in their mouths, and play music.

My own mouth was dry, and it tasted like the breath that I had once smelled on an epileptic. I got out of bed, went into the bathroom and washed it, and then killed the taste of the antiseptic with a glass of brandy. My stomach was empty, and I felt the liquor burn.

I washed my hands and went into the kitchen. A frying pan with bacon and eggs was on the range and a very small fire was burning under it. While I was putting the food on a plate, Myra came in.

"I went out for some scouring powder," she said, took her coat off and poured a cup of coffee for me.

"What time do you get out of here?" I said.

"About twelve o'clock—why?"

"Be on time; I have a date here."

"Will I be in the way?"

"Yes."

"You never worried about it before."

"I'm not worried."

"Why on time then?"

"This one is different."

"They're all alike."

"No."

"I used your own words," she said.

"I still say it."

"Then, how is she different?"

"She'd be embarrassed. Anyhow, how'd you know it was a she?"

"You have that kind of a look."

"What kind?"

"Never mind. I don't want to be insulting—your shirt is open."

I covered myself.

She gave me another cup of coffee and stood with her back against the sink and said: "Isn't it terrible about Mr. Tinevelli?"

"How'd you know?"

"Read it in this morning's papers."

"So they got it."

"Isn't it terrible? What made him do it?"

"What makes anybody do it?"

"What?"

"What made you do it?"

She became very red and her lips drew together in anger.

"I didn't say it to make you mad; I wanted you to know," I said, and when she did not answer . . . "I guess there's an excuse for everything."

Her face lost its hardness, and she said: "The old idea of friendship; it's beautiful. If you were a young man, you'd be cursing him for having imposed on you."

"Don't get mushy."

"No," she said slowly. "There's nothing mushy about you."

I wiped my mouth and got up, making sure my pajamas were not open.

"Will you be out of here on time?" I said.

Her face became hard again—hers was the most changeable face I had ever seen.

"Yes. I wouldn't spoil your fun for anything."

I dressed and went outside. It was very cold. The sun was bright but gave no warmth. The trees in the park were covered with icicles that glittered in the sunlight. When the wind blew, the branches rattled and the icicles snapped off and fell in a sparkling shower to the ground. I was very careful driving on the icy pavement.

The policeman at the station-house door was pushing an old woman out when I came up. She was cursing, and he was smiling.

"What's up?" I said.

"Nothing, sir. She's a little crazy."

"I'm not crazy," the woman said.

I looked at her. She was old and wrinkled and used a stick to support herself. There was only one tooth in her mouth; it was in her upper jaw and she kept running her lower lip and tongue over it. She also kept shifting from foot to foot, moving forward a few inches and then a few inches back.

"What's the matter?" I said.

"It's because I'm English they're throwing me out—the Irish." She looked at the policeman, and he grinned at her. "You don't hate the English, do you? You're not Irish?"

"No," I said.

"It's the Sullivan girls next to me. They say I'm running a whorehouse, and I'm not. They're running one. They say it because I'm English; and I say to them: 'Salisbart's a good name, even if it is an English name.' And they say to me, 'we're going to make war and kill all the English and all the Jews.' And I say, 'How would you like it if your father and brothers got killed?' They don't care; they're going to make war and kill all the English and the Jews."

While she was talking, she licked her tooth and shifted from foot to foot. I do not know why I listened to her. Did I like Jews? She did. They had given her the Bible and she was grateful. Did I read the Bible? Her mother had read it to her five times, and she always read it every day. God was everywhere, in the air, everywhere. Cause and effect, everything was cause and effect; and God saw everything. Her father, who had had rheumatism, had taken a piece of copper and a piece of lead and had put one in each shoe and had been cured. Electricity was God. Did I believe in God? I said, yes. I should appreciate everything, she said, because I was good-looking and must also have good-looking children. I'm not married, I said. Then, you will have good-looking children. She'd brought up two. She was beautiful once—you wouldn't think so. See this foot. God's punishment. When she was young, she had everything: horses, money, good-looks—why, when she'd pass, they'd turn around and say, isn't she beautiful! She hadn't appreciated it; she had thought it had been coming to her and should have it; everybody had it; so God had punished her. Cause and effect, again. Now, she appreciated everything; her heart was clean and good to everything. She had two little birds, and they sang all day. She'd say "sweet, who's sweet?" And they'd say "sweet-sweet"; she'd say, "who's going by-by?" and they'd say "by-by." I don't believe her. Her daughter hears it. Her daughter had a sore throat and the doctors said it was her tonsils, but she thought it was her teeth.

The policeman, who had gone inside when she had started to talk, came outside and said, "Telephone call for you, sir."

"I have to go," I said.

She began to speak again, but I turned around and went inside.

"Thanks," I said to the policeman. I knew there was no telephone call.

"She's cuckoo," he said.

I went up the wooden steps. Two plain-clothesmen were playing dice in the rest-room on the first floor. When they saw me, they scooped up the money and dice and began to talk. I walked past the doorway and went up to my office. Schlegel, the civilian clerk, was typewriting. He stopped when he saw me and took a package out of the drawer. It was wrapped in newspapers.

"A guy left it," he said.

"Who was it?"

"Dunno. He didn't say. Only said he was from the Apex Ticket Agency and he talked to you about it."

I picked up the package and went into the office and put it on the desk. I took off my hat and coat and hung it in the steel locker; and it occurred to me that taking your hat and coat off was like a Catholic prayer; you had to do it before everything.

I opened the package. There was lots of paper around it. With the last layers of paper around it, I could feel the gun of which the agency-man had spoken. I took the last layer off, and it was a Savage, .32 caliber, automatic pistol. I was disappointed, because I had imagined a small pocket pistol and had wanted it for my own use. I put the gun into the desk drawer and sat down.

Think; I did not want to think, because it would be too long to one o'clock. Beloved . . . beloved . . . I did not want to think about her.

Downstairs again, I talked to Mac. We talked of Wallace and the counterfeit tickets. He told me that he was getting along all right and had got back a lot of them, but that we would have to be goddam careful the night of the fight or there would be a stink raised that would reach to the Pope. I said, he was a fool; that, even if there was, we would not be connected with it. Anyway, nobody could say anything; we could threaten any possessor of a counterfeit with arrest.

I told him again that if Teeny was found, not to bring him in, but to let me know. (Keeping The Yid away had become more important than finding Teeny.)

I did a few things and occupied some time. About eleven o'clock, I went out to the barber-shop. The wind had died down and the chill had gone out of the air.

There is nothing that acts so good a sedative on a man as a barber-chair and a barber haircutting and shaving him. I lay back in the chair and enjoyed it; it was pleasant and was taking time.

At twelve, I was on my way uptown.

Thinking it was late, I asked the elevator-boy whether a lady had been upstairs for me, and he said: "No, sah, ain't been no lady," and smiled; his thick lips, creased with little black lines, smoothed out into plain purple when he smiled. He was still smiling when I left the elevator and went into my apartment.

I looked to see that everything was all right. I put out some wine and some brandy and two thin shell-glass glasses on a tray. The bedroom made me smile: a smile in which there was the beginnings of resentment. Myra had not put the spread on the bed and had turned the corner of the blanket down.

The bell rang, and I went and opened the door and she stood there. I took her arm, taking the full round arm into the palm of my hand, and walked with her into the parlor.

She looked around and said: "It's awfully nice"; and the words chased away the strangeness and we laughed.

She sat down on the couch. I stood over her and took the sides of her head in my hands and began to slip off her hat. She put her hands over mine and looked up at me. Her eyes were very deep, and I looked hard and saw deep into her.

"Let's go for a ride; it's so beautiful," she said.

"Too cold," I said. Jesus Christ, just when I get all set, she gets ideas, I thought.

I bent over and kissed her on the lips and she put her arms around me, so that, when I straightened, I lifted her up with me. Her face against mine, I felt a warm trickle on my neck. She was crying.

"A fine start," I said. "Why cry? We should be happy. You shouldn't be crying."

"How will it end?"

"Why worry about the end? We didn't even get started yet."

"I didn't think it could be so terrible."

"What's so terrible about it?"

"This. It hurts so much."

"What's hurting you?"

"Being . . . in love," she said, and she hesitated before she said the word "love."

"You're the one that's making it that way," I said.

"I would be happy if it wasn't the way it is."

"Don't think about anything but us."

"I can't help it. I had a terrible night. I didn't close my eyes."

"You're foolish. You'll have to stop being foolish. Life's too short to cry about things you should be happy about."

"I'll try. It's hardest when I start to think that I'm rotten."

"You're foolish. Could we help it? Is it our fault?"

"No, but where will it end?"

"Stop being so Jewish and looking backwards on everything."

"That's another thing."

"I'm starting to think you don't love me."

"How can you say that, Buck?"

"You make me. Why don't you look at it the way it should be and get everything you can out of it?"

"All right, I'm over it," she said and smiled.

"Let's drink on it."

"I don't drink, only a little wine on Passover."

"This is more important than Passover. Drink a little bit."

I poured two glasses of brandy. She put her lips to her glass and put it down again; I drank mine.

"Take your hat off," I said.

"Not here, I'll only start getting that rotten feeling."

I walked over to the piano and for a few seconds poked at the keys with my fingers, then turned around and said: "I'll take you to a nice place. We used to go when we were kids."

"Where?"

"We used to call it Pleasure Island."

"I'd like to go."

"You stay here; I'll get the car."

"I'd rather go with you."

"Have to come back for a blanket. There's no grass now and we want to sit down."

"I'll come with you and we can come back together. I don't want to wait here alone."

"Do it that way, then."

"I didn't think it could be so pretty so near the city," she said as I swung into the road that runs between the Zoo and the Botanical Gardens.

It was a grey day, not misty, but not very clear, and the small hills of the Gardens, which were studded with evergreens, looked nice against the grey sky. Out here, it did not seem as though winter touched at all; even the ground had a green-brown tinge.

We rode along, and the country became flat and there were no more evergreens, but the ground was a warm brown that looked soft and rich and inviting. A little distance from the sound, we could smell the breeze that came from there. In a little while, we crossed the bridge that went over the small strip of water which separated the island from the mainland. A railroad bridge ran along the side of the traffic bridge.

I went down the road a little and drove down an inclining side road to the railroad station and stopped at the deserted parking space.

"We walk the rest. No road," I said.

We got out, took the blanket and automobile robe and walked over the bridge which spanned the railroad and on to a cinder road. There were trees all along the road; they were naked. A breeze blew, but it was not cold.

We came suddenly out from among the trees, and the ground sloped sharply into a meadow. The cinder road did not go down to it, but was banked up level halfway across the meadow. They had intended to build it all the way across, but had abandoned the idea. We walked out on it, and we felt as though we were not of the earth. I ran down the sharp incline at the end and waited for her and caught her when she came down. We laughed.

The meadow was very low. Every step we made would squelch down, and the water would come up just enough to wet the bottom of our shoes.

Finally, we came to the hill on the other side of the meadow. The hill was covered with rocks and trees and brown earth. It was a steep climb. I helped her up to the top, and there before us was the Sound, restless and grey.

I spread the automobile robe under an overhanging rock where the earth was very dry, and she sat down on it.

"I have cinders in my shoes," she said.

I knelt and took her shoes off, shook them out, but did not put them back on her feet; instead, I covered her with the blanket, sat down and took my own shoes off.

"Put your feet under; they'll be cold," she said.

We lay there. She ran the tip of her index-finger along the hair on my temple. It felt good.

"You're very grey," she said.

"I'm very old."

"No. You're not old. You've had a lot of sorrow."

"Yes," I said and talked to her and told her about my childhood. I had never felt any sorrow over it, but I told it so she would sympathize.

"No parents at all would have been better. It's a wonder you came out of it so nice. Didn't she mother you at all?"

"No—and I didn't want it. I was mad, because the money that could've made it easier for me she gave to the church."

I looked at her and she got up on an elbow and looked over me at the Sound.

"I hate them for that," I said. "Always selling the idea of heaven: the more you pay, the nearer you get to the big-shot, God."

"You can't buy that."

"No."

"She was nearer to heaven than she knew," she said.

We did not talk much after that. She remained on her elbow, looking at the Sound and then said something very low.

"What?" I said.

She kept on a little louder: "'. . . from the depth of some divine despair.'"

"What's that?" I said.

"Something I learned in high-school."

"Say it all."

She said it. What the hell, I thought. I did not understand it.

XIII

The weather turned bad. It rained and snowed and then turned to rain again. When it did not rain, a heavy, damp mist would hang over the city and everything felt damp to the touch.

We met every day. Sometimes we would stay in; other times we would go riding. It was nice, with it warm in the car and the rain spattering on top of the car and on the windows. We did not speak much during the rides. Several times, we went to a play and sat with our knees touching; I did not enjoy them, because I kept thinking of being at home with her.

The Yid called me several times, but I told him that I was too busy to come out; that with the big fight and the search for Teeny I had no time. He asked for a "relief", but I told him that he was the only one whom I could trust with it, and that he owed me something for the soft job he had had all along. He was angry but did as I told him.

The night of the big fight, it became clear and cold. For the first time in weeks, the stars were bright in the sky and the streets were dry and clear of slush. During the day, I had gone down to see Wallace and had assured him that everything would be all right. I also told him that I wanted my share the next day; we came to an understanding as to the amount.

I went down to the Stadium early in the evening. The lines at the general admission gate went down the street to the avenue in back of the Stadium. The people in the front part of the line had been there all night. There were no reserved seats in the general admission, and first come were first served.

I had policemen and plain-clothes-men scattered over the entire neighborhood. The amount of policemen in front of the Stadium had driven the ticket-speculators to standing in front of the subway and elevated railway stations. They were picked up there. Orders had been given that the first man to release a speculator would be immediately tried and dismissed. It was a common practice to take a few dollars and let them go; but this time we put it strong. To the customers holding counterfeits, the crooked seal was shown and the tickets destroyed in their presence. If they objected, they were told politely that we would have to take them in for having counterfeits in their possession and they did not persist.

The crowds were coming in droves. They were held on the other side of the street by policemen until the traffic-lights stopped the heavy automobile traffic; then they would be released at one time and come in a solid mass. We had both the riot and the bomb squads out.

There was a squad of mounted policemen lined up in front of the curb just before the Stadium. Captain Mac, in full uniform, was there, too. They were waiting for the arrival of the Mayor. No taxicabs or private cars were permitted to stop there; they had to go on to the next street and unload. Pedestrians were ordered off the street, and only those holding tickets were permitted on the street, and they had to go in directly. The manager of the chain drug-store, which had an entrance on the street and in the Stadium, came out and protested that we were driving his regular neighborhood customers away; he was told to make a formal complaint. He went back into the store very angry.

I did not wait for the Mayor to arrive but went in, and the Stadium was almost full then. It was a mass of faces. Because of the smoke and dim lights—the first preliminary was just going on and the only light was that above the ring—it seemed unreal. It was like a hornets' nest that buzzed and buzzed; only once in a while you could distinguish a distinct, individual voice, and that was close by or when someone shouted louder than the hum.

Of the preliminaries, I do not remember much. Except for one little fighter, it was just pure slugging. He—the little one— was perfect. He kept his fists up and kept boring in and cutting the other to pieces. There was not a wasted motion. It was beautiful. He did not have enough punch to put his opponent out, but he systematically and deliberately wore him down to quivering piece of bleeding flesh. The only thing which spoiled it for me was the woman behind me shouting into my ear for the little fellow to cut the other man's ear off— she would not be satisfied with anything less than an ear. It was a performance that should have been admired in silence.

The Mayor had come in and the crowd had duly roared. He sat in the row in front of me. I was in the second row, the end seat. When the lights went up before the main bout, he turned and saw me. He got up and motioned me to come over. I went up to him and we walked a few steps to the corner of the ring where there were no reporters. The crowd, seeing him on his feet, cheered. In the cheering, we were alone.

"Why didn't you come down?" he said.

"I was waiting for you."

"Mike told me."

I shrugged my shoulders.

"If you think you have anything on me, I'll go the full way with you," he said. "I'm doing it because it's good politics. It's a good idea: policeman works way up to Commissioner—the reward of virtue. But not now. They'll say, I don't know my own mind: make a commissioner and break him in no time. Later in the term, he'll resign, and it's yours."

"I waited so long, a little time more wouldn't kill me," I said.

Tierney and his handlers came down the aisle, and we had to get out of the way. They climbed into the ring. The Mayor and I shook hands and went to our seats. The Champion came into the ring on the other side.

The referee got into the ring, and I saw Wallace jump up, excited. The front rows, where all the big gamblers sat, began to buzz with excitement. Wallace went over to a white-haired man sitting in the front row. He kept speaking to him, and the old man kept shaking his head. One gambler stood up and shouted at the top of his voice that all bets were off with him. The gallery came back with cries to throw the bum out.

Wallace saw that it was useless arguing; he shrugged his shoulders and went back to his seat. The changed referee was to remain. The lights went down.

The pictures of the fighters were taken and the referee had them in the center of the ring, giving them their instructions, when someone touched my shoulder. I looked up.

"We found Tinevelli." It was Captain MacDunn speaking.

"What!"

"We found him."

"Where've you got him?"

"Boarding-house on Landis Street. He took the pipe."

The bell clanged; the fighters shuffled into the center of the ring—so Teeny was through. . . .

I got up slowly.

"Who knows it?" I said.

"Me, Reilly on the desk, and the cop I sent out—and I guess the hospital people."

"How'd you know?"

We walked up the aisle; the people about began to shout, "Sit down!"

"A priest, a Father MacLaughlin, called in."

"How in hell'd he know?"

"Search me."

"What's the number?"

"Three sixty-seven."

"You stay here," I said. "Maybe there'll be trouble. They switched referees, and the sports might start something. Boxing Commission maybe got wise to the referee fixing. Wallace tried to talk 'em out of it, but no go."

All the way, the words of the poem that Beth had so absently spoken in her hoarse voice that day on the island kept running through my mind; but if someone had asked me to say it, I could not. It was nothing definite, only a feeling that I was hearing it again and understanding.

The house was not very far. It was near the river and was on one of the city streets that had not changed with the times: frame houses stood on high terraces. I ran up the stone steps and walked across the small lawn to the house and rang the bell. The policeman let me in.

The hallway was narrow. A wide doorway leading into the parlor was on one side. An elderly woman and two girls were standing in the doorway. I could hear a radio broadcasting the fight; they had forgotten to turn it off. That was the only sound. There was the faint smell of gas.

"Where is he?" I asked the policeman.

"Top floor back, sir. Father MacLaughlin is there."

The woman came over and began to cry and said: "It isn't my fault."

"Anybody say it was?"

"We're a respectable family. It's the first time we let out a room."

"Don't you run a boarding-house?"

"No, sir. Only one room. It helped."

"Know who he is?"

"Mr. Ripley?"

"All right. Keep your mouth shut and nobody'll be wiser. We'll get him out of here in no time," I said. I was glad she did not know who Teeny was.

I went upstairs to the top floor. The door was open, and I walked into the room. Father MacLaughlin sat at the small table in the center of the room; crumpled toilet-paper was all over the floor—Teeny must have used it to stuff the cracks in the door and window; what was left of Teeny was on the bed. There was a gold crucifix on his chest and it glowed a dull red in the shaded light.

Father MacLaughlin got up.

"How do?" he said.

"How'd you know?" I said.

I turned my back to him and walked to the bed and looked at Teeny. His skin was bluish red and splotchy all over and his face muscles were drawn together so that it looked as though he was grinning. It was not nice.

"He called me by telephone," the priest said.

"He what?"

"He spoke to me while he was dying."

I looked around. There was a telephone on the wall.

"It's an extension," the priest said.

"Why didn't you hang up right away and trace the call?"

"It was my choice: either to take a chance and get the police too late or to shrive him over the phone; and I chose to save his soul."

I looked down at Teeny and said: "A hell of a lot you saved."

We did not say anything for a while, then: "Where'd he get gas?"

The priest pointed to a pipe sticking out of the wall.

"He took the cap off. It's a disconnected pipe."

"And they didn't smell it downstairs?"

"No."

"When did you get here?"

"Just as the hospital people were leaving. They couldn't do anything with him, so they left him for the coroner."

"What about burying him? You owe him something," I said.

"We should be able to do something. For that matter I shouldn't have shriven him either. That was personal."

"What's the difference," I said. "It doesn't make any difference. There's worms in ground that's not consecrated."

"If there was no charge against him, I could say he was demented."

"I'll squash the charge."

"It can be managed."

"Leave the arrangements to you—you can make the statement to the papers. You tell his family; I won't," I said.

There was quiet again.

"Well, I'm going," I said and walked towards the door.

"Inspector," he said.

I turned around.

"I'd forgotten; he left a note for you."

The priest took a letter out of the book and handed it to me. I opened the envelope; the priest turned away and walked back to the table. The letter was in Teeny's writing and read:

> *Buck: I guess I'm finished and this is the one way, I figure, is left. My property can cover the bank and my insurance can cover the family.*
>
> *If I'm dead, they won't be so foolish as to come out with it. I know only one, and he's the go-between. Of course, his name is John Smith. He is tall and would look like a drug addict,—only his face is all covered with small pink freckles and it gives him a false flush. There's a cold sore on the right side of*

his mouth that I think is chronic, because I never saw him without it. Another way, perhaps, you could find him. I always called Landseer 6880. They always answered as a sanitarium for women. It's a private line. I tried to get the phone company to give me the address, but they wouldn't do it.

Get the bastards if you can without messing me up. So long. Teeny.

I felt myself get cold all over and an inside chill began to shake me. I clenched my teeth to keep them from hitting against each other; and I went over to the telephone and spoke to the operator.

"There's a line being held open for police use in the drugstore in the Stadium—yes, right in the same building. I want it. This is Inspector Safiotte. All right, I'll hold on."

I leaned up against the wall. The priest looked up from his Bible and then looked down again and turned the page. The room swayed slowly before me from side to side. After a minute, I heard the buzzing at the other end and some one answered.

"This is Inspector Safiotte," I said. "Are you the patrolman stationed on the phone?"

"Yes, sir," he said. "Patrolman Lunde."

"Get Captain MacDunn. He'll, maybe, be in my seat: section D, second row, ringside."

"He's outside here. The fight's over. Semi-final on, now."

"Get him."

When Mac came to the telephone, I said: "Get that damn head of yours on this. It's in this precinct and it's a screwy deal and you should know. Telephone connection Landseer is in this precinct, no? Landseer 6880. Well, you should know. Know anybody looks like a dopey except for pink freckles all over his mug and wears a cold sore on the right side of his mouth? Tall guy, thin—if I knew his name, would I be asking you? John Smith, naturally. For Chrissake get that head of yours working."

His voice came slowly over the wire: "Maybe it's Salmon. Call him Salmon because of the pink freckles."

"Who's he?"

"Runs a speakeasy on Sidelle Street near Blake. One of the boys. He's all right. That's about his measure—not his phone number, though."

"Private line. Think he'll be there?"

"Sure. Big night, tonight," he said.

"Bring him in."

"What for?"

"I got a few questions to ask, that's all."

"All right."

"Think we could do anything with the telephone people?" I asked.

"You know how those bastards are."

"All right, Mac. Get him in. Maybe I'll be late, but you wait."

"You know, Tierney lost the fight," he said.

"To hell with that," I said and hung up. "So-long," I said to the priest and walked to the door. "Say, hold that statement to the press—don't even tell his family. Get him to an undertaker that can keep his mouth shut. I'll tell you when to spring it. I'll fix the coroner, just tell him I know the dead one's people."

"Why?"

"I'm going to get the guys responsible. What name did you give the hospital people?"

"None. They must have given it to them, downstairs."

"Good."

"You can get me at the University."

I took the patrolman with me when I went outside.

"You go with me. If we get into a traffic jam, blow your whistle. We're going for a ride."

He stood on the running-board. I started the car and drove up the river street and around into the cross streets to the park. We went at a fast clip through it, swinging close around the curves. The streets were clear now, and the patrolman opened the door, swung inside and sat down. On the bridge across the river, the draw-bridge was open and we had to wait at the barrier. A tug passed, the black smoke making the green and red lamps on its masts seem to blink. Finally, when the draw was back, we crossed and I put on speed again.

The telephone company building was at the tip of two crossing streets and was built in a triangle. Flood lights lighted up the dome and the company flag on it. I drove up and stopped at the door.

"You stay here," I said and got out of the machine and went to the dimly lighted doorway. When I went in, two men were there. One was sitting at the desk which was close to the rail that cut off the open office from the hallway. The other, the night watchman—he had the time punch hanging by a strap around his neck—was leaning over the rail. They were talking, and straightened up when they saw me.

I walked to the desk. The young man stood up. "Yes, sir?" he said.

"I'm a police inspector." I showed my badge.

"Yes, sir?"

"About a year ago—no, more like sixteen months—you had a girl working for you: Dace Clarke. She was in the long distance department, night work."

"Just a moment."

He went to a filing cabinet and looked among the cards and came back with one.

"She's on duty, now," he said. "Anything wrong?"

"No, nothing like that. Just personal. I want to see her."

"It's not customary . . ."

"I want to see her," I said sharply.

He looked at me and then down at his hand on the rail.

"Come this way, please," he said at his hand and swung the gate open.

I followed him. He opened the door to a room, went in and put on the light. I went in after him. The room was furnished with wicker furniture.

"Sit down, sir," he said.

"I'll stand."

He went out and I heard him speaking by telephone. I waited. It certainly was quiet. The noise upstairs was sort of shut away from here. There was a *Red Book* on the table. I picked it up, then put it down again. Dace stood in the doorway. She came in, stopped, and came further in.

"Look who's here," she said; and when she stood in front of me, she said again: "Look who's here."

"Hello, Dace," I said.

"The big fella, himself. What brings the big fella on a night call on a poor working girl?"

"Cut it out and sit down."

She sat down, the green working smock coming open over her knees as she crossed them. The smock would not close when she tried it, so she covered her knee with her hand. I stood over her.

"You're getting fat, Buck," she said.

I instinctively drew in my belly.

"What brought on this?" she said.

"I'd like a favor," I said.

The flesh of her knee bulged up between her spread fingers as she squeezed her hand down hard. She laughed a little and said: "That's just like you: kick somebody in the pants and then come around and ask a favor." She laughed again. "And the funny part is that you get it."

"This is important."

"Nothing but dames is important to you."

"I was sincere," I said.

"Guess you were—at the time."

"I was."

"Well, what d'you want?"

I spoke low. "I want an address; I got a number. It's a private line."

"And get the can tied to me? Nix."

"Nobody'll know."

"Not my department."

"You know the girls," I said.

She thought a while. Then: "Why the hell should I?"

"It's important."

The fingers on her knee curved up again and then flattened out and began to smooth the flesh.

"Shove that phone over here," she said.

I pushed the French telephone on the table nearer her. She picked it up and called an extension.

"Is that you, Lou?" she asked. "This is Dace. Want to see you. Meet me in the toilet right away."

After putting the phone down very slowly, she got up and said: "What a damn fool I am—what's the number?" I told her. "Wait, I'll be back." She went out.

I walked around the room several times. The young man came to the door, looked in, and went back to his desk. Dace came back and said we would have to wait. She refused my offer of a chair. I walked up to her and said: "I appreciate this. I won't forget it."

"No, you won't. It's all right. Never mind the thanks."

The neck of her smock was low. There were several small white scars on the upper part of her breast.

"Still shows," I said.

She looked down at my hands and said: "Still have sharp nails?"

"I didn't know they were sharp till you hollered."

She pulled the smock up a little and covered the scars.

"I got a boy-friend, now."

"That's nice," I said.

"He's a Swede, a square-head and dumb, but . . ."

"That's nice, that's damn nice."

"Oh, shut up."

The telephone bell rang and she answered it. "Thanks, darling," she said and hung up. To me: "112 Sidelle Street."

"I guess that's near Blake," I said. "Thanks, I appreciate it."

"He's a square-head and he's all right—but after you . . . Get the hell out of here before I tell you what a lousy skunk you are."

I went.

They were there, smoking cigarettes and talking to the desk-sergeant when I came in. Mac introduced me to Salmon.

"Hello," I said. "Come on upstairs. You stay here, Mac."

"He's all right," Mac said. "One of the boys." Then to Salmon: "The inspector is all right."

We went upstairs. I put on the light in the office, snapped on the green-shaded desk light, and put out the big center light again.

I sat down at the desk; Salmon sat at the other side.

"How's business?"

"Not so hot," he said.

I smiled and said: "Afraid we'll ask for a bigger cut?"

"No; it's not so hot."

"Want to ask a few questions."

"Anything inside of reason."

"Ever in the women's sanitarium business?"

He fidgeted a little and said: "We need a private line for good customers. That's the way we talk. Then we can deal in cases."

I looked hard at him and did not say anything for a minute; then: "Salmon, how much did you get out of the Tinevelli racket?"

His face was splotchy yellow, now under the green light it became greenish-grey, and he got up.

"I don't get you."

"Once more. Who thought it up and bossed the frame?"

"So help me, I don't get you."

"Once more," I said and got up slowly and stood with the palms of my hands flat on the desk. "Opening up?"

"I don't get you." He had been so surprised that he could think of nothing else to say.

I brought my right hand up from the desk, clenching it as it came up, and swung the fist crosswise with all my force. My big signet ring cut his cheek open, and I felt the bone in his nose give as my fist caught it on the side.

He swayed back a little and drew his breath in slowly; it rattled in his throat. The blood was running from his nose and, as he breathed in, it choked him and he coughed. A fleck of blood hit me in the face; I wiped it away. His eyes closed, and he suddenly sat down on the chair and his head fell forward on the desk. The blood flowed and was absorbed in a widening blot by the green blotting-pad on the desk.

There was no movement for several minutes, so I went into the toilet, took a towel, and soaked it in cold water, and came back. I hit him a few smacks on the back of the head. He stirred, and I pushed him up against the back of the chair. His head fell back and he opened his eyes.

"You can hear me?" I said.

It took a big effort, but he nodded.

"Who?" I said.

"Wait a minute," he managed to get out.

I waited. He lifted his head; his nose was way over on the side.

"They'll kill me for it," he said, and I had difficulty in understanding him.

"They wouldn't know. All I want's the name. I'll work on him, and when I get through . . ."

"Lester," he said.

"Lester?" I juggled the name in my mind. "Martin Lester, the one who was partners with 'Big Stem James' in the nightclub business in Quebec?"

"I don't know about James, but his first name's Martin."

"That's him all right," I said. "Funny how all you rats are just like one big family. Put a finger in the manure pile and pull one of you out and trace back on you, and you spread out and connect up somewhere. You pal up, bust up because you trust each other so much, and pal up with somebody else again, and you're in every low down, dirty deal from plugging up telephone slots to walking out on a two-bit whore without paying her.— Well, what's the story?"

He said something, choked up, and spat a blob of blood.

"What, what?" I said. "Get the manure out of your mouth so I can understand you."

"Jesus," he said and began to cry. "You hand me a sock like this and expect me to talk straight."

"Go ahead and talk."

"Don't blame me. I didn't know about it till after. I only handled it for Lester. He told me."

"Dry your eyes. How'd they pick on Tinevelli?"

"Lester saw an article in the paper how everybody trusted him and he was the big cheese in the bank." He spat again. "And a wop's easy to lay for with a good-lookin' woman."

"Who's the dame?"

"She ain't here no more. Lester tended to that—what a picture! The wop was—aw, I guess she made him do it; a drunk ain't responsible."

"What was your split?"

"Five percent."

"Who are the rest?"

"Don't know. Lester's the big boss—I only know that."

"Bitch!—Suppose Lester knew about the family?"

He bent over to spit, and when I said, "Spit in the damn towel," he looked at me with reproach and let it dribble from his mouth into the towel on the desk.

"Did he figure the family?" I repeated.

"Sure he figured on that. It was in the article all about them."

I sat down and picked up the receiver of the telephone.

"Reilly," I said.

"Yes, sir."

"Get Dr. Raider out of bed and tell him to come over. If he isn't home, leave a message for him. Do the same thing with Judge Campiglia; tell him to bring a blanket warrant for grand larceny. I'm swearing it."

"Yes, sir."

I hung up.

"The doctor'll patch you up. You don't have to be afraid; nobody's going to know."

"Thanks—he'll kill me," he said, and tried to wipe the blood away from his face.

I said: "Put the wet towel on your face; it'll stop the blood and ease up the pain. Doc'll be here soon."

He picked up the wet towel and put it against his face. I bent down and took a bottle out of the desk-drawer.

"You better take a drink," I said.

He shook his head. I took a drink.

"Be back in a minute," I said and went out of the room. I wanted to give him a chance to get the charge of narcotic I knew he was aching for.

XIV

It was five in the morning when I was through at the station-house. The doctor had come and patched up Salmon. We bedded him down in one of the cells. I told him that he could leave any time he wanted to. He said that he would sleep a little and then go home.

Judge Campiglia had not come. He probably had been at the fight and was ending up by making a night of it. It was all right, except that I had waited for him; I could get the warrant the next day.

I did not feel as though I wanted to go home and go to sleep. The desire to go and talk with Beth came over me. I tried to fight it off; then, I could not see why I should not. It would take me an hour to get there and six in the morning was not an unusual hour.

It became light while I was driving uptown. There was no traffic and it was very nice driving along, first in darkness, then in dim light, and into the daylight. I had the window open and the cold air rushed against my face. Later, uptown, I passed big trucks bringing produce from the farms down to the city. They rumbled past, and the drivers looked tired and cold.

I rang the bell a short ring; there was no answering buzz. After ringing a few times, the buzz came and I went in and up and rang the door-bell.

"Who's there?" she said, speaking low.

"Me, Buck," I said.

The lock snapped and she opened the door. I went in. She was in her kimono.

"What do you want, Buck? So early."

"I want to talk to you."

"So early?" she said.

I saw she was irritated at my early visit.

"Couldn't it have waited?" she went on.

"I wanted to talk to you bad."

She turned around and went down the hallway; I followed her.

"Sit down," she said, and went into the bathroom.

I heard her washing her mouth. Presently, she came out and sat down next to me on the sofa. She had a hair-brush in her hand.

"What did you want?" she said.

I leaned over and kissed her on the mouth, and it tasted of tooth-paste. I ran my fingers down her hair. It was long and soft and a rich brown.

"What did you want to say?" she said and leaned back and began to brush her hair. She was very vain about her hair.

Beginning from the first of the affair, I told her about Teeny. I wanted her to understand, even though I was only talking to relieve myself. Maybe I was brutal in telling it, but I was not acting now; I had nothing to gain, and I could not put anything into my voice. All I wanted was to get it out of me to someone who would feel the same about it as I did.

When I finished, she stopped brushing her hair and said: "I don't pity him; I pity his wife."

I became angry, because I saw she was acting like a woman.

"He didn't want pity," I said.

"He was a coward."

"*You* think so."

"What do you think?"

"It was deliberate. He was goddamn game."

"What about the rest of it?"

"He couldn't help it. Any man would've done the same thing," I said. I had not told her how bad the picture had been.

"How could he say that he loved his wife and yet do that?"

"You can."

"Impossible."

"Don't be a woman."

"That's the trouble with men: they show clean on the outside and are dirty inside."

I was very angry and said: "What about yourself?"

She became very white; her underlip began to quiver, and then her lips drew together in a thin, straight line. She nodded her head and said: "I expected that, sometime. Yes, I expected that."

"I didn't mean that. I was mad."

"I expected it when you'd get angry."

"Let's forget it!"

"No. Henry will have to come back anyway."

"He wouldn't know."

"You can't have me on the side."

"How about a divorce?"

She looked at me a long moment. "You don't even know yourself," she said. "You actually think that. You know better."

"That's a hell of a way to talk after you tell me you love me."

"That's the funny part of it; I do."

"Well, what's the idea?"

"I don't think you'll ever understand. It can only come to a rotten end, and I'll be the one to get the rotten end."

"It don't have to end rotten. You can leave him, and I'll frame him."

"No, Buck." Her voice became soft. "Even if I was free, I wouldn't marry you."

"What a hell of a note."

"There's no use talking any more. It's over between the two of us."

"It isn't," I said, getting up.

"You can't be that way with me." She was still talking quietly.

"I'll tell The Yid," I said.

"You won't. You think too much of your position."

"To hell with that!"

"Perhaps not now, but after a good sleep, you will."

"I won't."

"Go ahead, get some sleep—send for Henry."

"Anxious for a change?"

"Don't be insulting, Buck. You can't make me feel any worse than I do."

"You're anxious for a change," I said.

"Well, if this will settle it—I'm a whore. I might as well say it; I feel like one."

"You need the sleep. I woke you and you're mad."

"You think this is a sudden decision because I'm angry?"

"It's all of a sudden."

"I'm not angry."

"You are."

"No. The first few days were beautiful, then I started to think."

"Think what?"

"What's the use! You couldn't know. You'd better kiss me good-bye."

"I'll give you more than a kiss." I thought to excite her.

"Nothing but a kiss."

"I'll give you nothing."

While I stood looking at her, she looked at the carpet and then began to brush her hair slowly. I picked up my hat and coat and went out.

I went into the corner drug-store, called the station-house and talked to Captain Mac over the telephone.

"Call up Tinevelli's—you know the number—and tell that damn Jew to come back. Stick him on a beat," I said.

"Pounding pavement?"

"Yes—wait a minute! Goddamn it, no! Tell him to take the day off and go home. I'll see him tomorrow."

"What's up, Chief?"

"Nothing," I said and hung up.

It was still very early, and there was little traffic on the street. I went along, driving as fast as I could. When I got home, Myra was there already.

"You weren't home all night?" she said.

"No," I said and went into the parlor and drank half a drinking-glass of cognac. I sat down; and Myra, standing in the doorway, said: "What's the matter?"

"Nothing."

"There is."

"Nothing. I'm thirsty."

"You never drink that way."

"You goddamn women," I said and took another drink.

"Don't do that!"

"What the hell do you care?"

"Buck, don't do that!"

"Oh, shut up," I said, and drank again.

She came over and put her hand on my shoulder.

"What happened?" she said.

"Shut up! Oh, shut up!"

"Tell me," she said and put her hand on my forehead.

"You goddamn women."

The liquor made me want to cry, and I could not; and suddenly the couch slid out from under me and Myra was helping me up from the floor.

"Better get into bed," she said.

"I got something important to do today. I got . . ."

"You're sick and didn't sleep all night, Buck," she said.

"I got to fix that bitch, Martin Lester."

"Come on, Buck, go to bed. Leave it."

She helped me into the bedroom and helped me off with my clothes. I was very sleepy, and with the dark shades down, I went to sleep immediately. How long I slept, I do not know, but I was awake and the bed was tilting up on a side and I slid off on to the floor. The floor began to move up in the same way.

Myra came in and gave me a hand into the bathroom. I vomited and felt better. After that, I slept.

It was dark when I got up. My stomach felt empty and I had a rotten taste in my mouth. I took a drink of Strega di benevento, sipping it slowly so that it would not make me sick. Dressed, I filled the long, silver flask with the liquor and went out and had something to eat.

It did not make any difference to me where I went, so I told the taxicab driver to take me anywhere. While we drove downtown, I took several drinks from the flask. I felt pretty good when we pulled up before a small door in a side street of the theatrical district.

I got out, paid the driver, and looked around. I was in my own district and not very far from the station-house and in front of a night-club.

The doorman pushed the door open for me and I went in. The stairway was steep and curved around to the right. I steadied myself and went slowly down the steps into the lobby.

I gave my hat and coat to the check-girl and said: "How's business?"

"Another slow night. It's getting to be a habit."

A man was talking in the telephone-booth under the stairs. The person on the other end of the line probably did not hear him, because he shouted: "Tell him to open the store for me tomorrow; I won't be home. No, I won't be home."

"Hicks on a holiday," the check-girl said.

"Yeah, hicks," I said.

I pushed open the swinging doors; two acrobats were performing on the dancing-floor in the center, and the chorus was sitting along the sides on the floor. The music was not playing. A waiter came up and took me to a table near the dancing-floor. There were a lot of empty tables; it was slow. I gave the waiter an order for a small steak.

My left knee almost touched the back of the girl sitting on the floor near my table. I noticed that she was twisting and saw that a shoulder strap had torn and that she was trying to keep her dress from slipping down. I took the collar-pin out of my soft collar and tapped her on the shoulder.

"Here y'are, sister," I said.

She took it, smiled at me, and tried to pin her strap to the dress, but the tear was in the back. I reached down and took the pin out of her hand and pinned it for her.

"Thanks," she said and smiled.

Two men and two women came in and sat down at the table next to mine. The back of the man toward me was familiar. He must have felt me staring at him, because he turned around; I recognized the doctor who had x-rayed me.

"Hello, Inspector," he said. "Come and sit down here."

I went over.

"Meet the girls," he said.

"Some more cousins," I said, and he laughed.

"This is Martin Baylis. He teaches the art of writing poetry in the Metropolitan University," he said, introducing the man with him.

"No kidding!" I said, and the doctor laughed.

Martin Baylis looked at me coldly, turned to the girl and began to talk to her. I heard him say something about "his style." He was continuing his conversation. All the time that I was joking with the doctor and the girl, the poet kept up his talk. The girl with him looked bored and sometimes could not keep from laughing at something we said. After a while, Baylis got a few drinks into himself and stopped talking about his style and started on his inspiration. He was better at that.

"It's slow tonight," the doctor said.

"You talk like you been here often," I said.

"Let's go over to my place," he said.

"I haven't got a girl," I said.

"That's nothing," he said, but I could see that he was not pleased that I did not have one.

"Wait a minute," I said.

The chorus was doing a dance, and when it ended, I stopped the girl whose dress I had pinned and asked her if she wanted to go with us.

"I'd like to," she said, "but I'm stuck here till three."

"You tell the manager I want to see him."

She went through the swinging doors on the side of the room. In a minute, she came back to the door and pointed me out to the short man with her. He came over.

"You know me?" I said.

"Who doesn't in this business, Inspector?" he said.

"Can she go?"

"She's getting ready now. Is there something else?" he said, his little moustache wagging up and down as he spoke.

"You got any liquor up your place?" I asked the doctor.

"Plenty," he said and laughed loudly. He was a little drunk.

"No," I said to the manager. "Nothing else."

"Any time, Inspector, any time you want good stuff."

"I'll remember," I said.

He went back through the swinging doors, and the chorus-lady came out. We all got up.

"What's your name?" I asked.

"Lucille."

I introduced her and we trooped out, stopping to get our hats and coats from the check-girl. The doctor drove his own car; the ride was a miracle of drunken luck.

We all got out of the car in front of the hotel. The doctor opened the door, and we went in, left our coats downstairs in the waiting-room and went up the stairs in single file; the stairs were too narrow for two to walk abreast. We went through the cold, white tiled office and into the room beyond. It was past reality. One minute you were cold and frightened, and the next you were warm and soothed. The room was like that.

The doctor called us into the alcove and told us to gather around a small door. He opened the door, pressed a button, and there was a miniature barroom; there was the bar with a brass-rail, the back-bar with glassware and silverware. We all talked and laughed and admired. We lined up in front of the bar, and the doctor lifted the flap at the end and went behind it and opened a locker in the back-bar in which there were all shapes of bottles standing around a refrigerator.

"Watch this," he said.

He took out several bottles,—I recognized Vermouth, Benedictine, Crême de Cocoa, Crême de Menthe,—and poured some of each into a glass, pouring it slowly so that one color would overlay the next and not mix with it. He made one of these for each of us; while we talked a mile to the minute.

"Drink it slowly," he said.

We lifted our glasses; here's looking at you, happy days, many of them. We drank slowly so we would not mix the flavors. I drank mine watching the others. First the green disappeared, then the red, then the green, and last the brown. It was fine.

After drinking several more, we took a few bottles and went out into the other room and sat down. The girl with Martin Baylis wanted to sit on his lap; he pushed her off and said: "No woman ever inspired a poet."

She said, "Aw, nuts," and tried to sit down again.

"No woman ever inspired a poet," he said loudly again.

Lucille came over to me and sat down next to me and put her head on my chest and her arms around me. I put my arms around her, closed my eyes, and held her tight against me. My love, my true love—my love tonight was lying close to someone else, her breasts pressed flat against somebody else's chest—drink her down, damn, drink her down. . . .

I pushed Lucille away, got up quickly and went over to the radio and slammed my fist down several times so that the candlesticks bounced. Baylis came over to me and put his arm around me and said: "What's the matter, boy? Sweet boy, so sad."

I gave him a push and said: "Get the hell away from me, you damn faggot."

He had caught my wrist. "Look at this boy's wrist," he said and circled it with his fingers.

I pulled my arm away.

Baylis switched on the radio, and as it began to play, Lucille and the doctor danced. The two girls were arguing drunkenly over something.

"No poet was ever inspired by a woman," Baylis said.

"Shut up, Pansy," I said. "I'm going home."

Nobody noticed or cared when I went out.

XV

My head the next day felt like a blown-up balloon that was trying to fly away and was being held down by my body. But I felt better about it. There was left only the effort to keep myself from showing the hatred for him.

When I walked into the station-house, Captain Mac met me in the desk room; he was excited, which was not ordinary with him.

"What do you think about it?"

"Think about what?" I said.

"Didn't you get it?"

"No."

"Stein got his last night."

"That baby was riding for a flop. How'd they hand it to him?"

"Last night, he gets out of his taxi and the taxi drives away. Somebody walks up to him, shoves a gun against the back of his head and lets fly. The taxi driver stops and sees a guy duck around the corner, and like a wise bird, he beats it for the station-house. When the doorman gets outside, Stein's as dead as his grandmother's great-aunt. We been picking up everything on the stem. I guess you know how good that is."

"I'm glad it's not in our district."

"Yeah, thank God!"

"Thank the bird that plugged him. I wonder what the little lady will do—I guess that's out."

"What little lady?"

"That baby-girl Stein played with."

"He ain't the only one."

"You know about it?"

"Sure. Every flatfoot knows."

"And I thought I had a good thing."

"Sure, everybody knows it and they were all getting set to land on him. Wallace's running around with her, too. He's got a yellow girl—and ain't she a beaut?—in an apartment on Rider, and he switches off once in a while with the kid. Mixes his drinks."

"The dirty scum."

"You said it."

"You're lucky, Mac."

"I guess, figuring that way, I am."

"Figuring any way, you're lucky."

"All right, I'm lucky. Something's eating you."

"Nothing's eating me."

"You thought before that it was tough."

"You're a dumb Scotchman. You're dumb like all Scotchmen. Sure it's tough, and it's lucky."

"What the hell?"

"You dumb Scotchman. It's wonderful and sometimes, when you can't get it the way you want, it's like something trying to tear your guts out."

"The way you want it?"

"For me, the one I want; for guys like Wallace and Stein, the other is reserved."

"If I could, anybody would be all right," he said.

"You're all right, Mac. Come on up and have a drink. My head feels like it's going to break into a hundred pieces."

"Judge Campiglia's upstairs; he was here twice yesterday. Your woman called up and said you were sick and wouldn't be here till this morning. I told him to come in today."

"The Judge is okey. Come on up."

We went upstairs. The Judge was sitting in the outside room. He got up, and we shook hands and went inside, Captain Mac walking after us. The Yid was sitting in a chair propped up against the wall. He had a cigarette in his mouth.

"Hello, chief," he said, and the cigarette clinging to his underlip bobbed up and down as he spoke.

"'Lo, Yid," I said. "Sit down, Pete." This to the judge.

He sat down. I got the bottle and set up the drinks, and we drank.

"I'll be going downstairs," Mac said.

"Take Levinson with you, Mac. This is private."

Mac motioned to The Yid, and they went out. I did not talk right away, but sat there and listened to the sound of their footsteps going down the wooden steps.

"How's tricks?" Judge Campiglia asked.

"Pretty good, Pete. How's life with you?"

"Good."

"That's good."

We had known each other a long time, living together in Little Italy. When I was offered the opportunity of buying the sergeancy, he bought his way past the Bar. We came in contact with each other in the courts, but that is where it ended. There is nothing in the world like an Italian who has money and a profession.

Did he have the warrant? Yes, he had, he said. There it was all set for signing. Yes, I had a case, I said and told him about Teeny. That was hardly a case, he said; the word of a "dopey." It maybe would not go so good with the jury. I said it was all right, because, when I got Mr. John Doe, I would have a confession. We spoke about "squashing" the warrant against Teeny. He said that he would fix it; restitution could always fix a first offense. Would he have another drink? Yes, he would. Luck, lots of luck! Good liquor, very good liquor. It was difficult to get good liquor. Yes, I guessed it was. Well, he would be going. Sorry, damned sorry about Teeny; he'd fix it sure. Thanks, I said, thanks a hell of a lot. Good-bye, good-bye.

I followed him into the outside room, and he said good-bye again and went downstairs.

"Schlegel," I said to the civilian clerk. "You been in my desk for anything?"

"No, sir. Not since . . ."

"All right. Ring downstairs and tell Captain Mac to hop up here."

I went into the office and pretty soon Captain Mac came in.

"You know, Mac, giving it a think, I don't think there's going to be a hell of a lot of holler about Stein. The old man won't let anything come out. They were like this—so close. The papers'll knock till something else comes up and that'll end it. Too much about Stein might come out."

"Before you hit Wallace, you better wait anyway till it gets quiet."

"He's all right; he'll pay."

"Sure he's all right, but I guess he got nicked plenty. Changed referee hit a lot of guys heavy and it don't take much heavy thinking to lay the Stein kill to one of those guys."

"I wonder who."

"They'll all have a sweet alibi."

"Well, what the hell!"

"Sure," Captain Mac said and went out.

The Yid came in and sat down and said, "Did you find him?"

"Who? Find who?"

"Tinevelli. The old lady got all excited when I told her I was through. Did we find him? And how was he? When would she see him? I told her to lay off; that I got my orders and damn glad to get home; that I didn't know nothing about it. Lately, it got so as I couldn't stand it. If I see another greasy wop meal, I'll vomit. Did you find him?"

"We found him all right. He took the pipe."

The Yid whistled a long whistle and said: "That poor fat slob. Wait till she hears it. She's nuts about him."

I shrugged my shoulders, picked up the reports on my desk, and began to read them. The Yid sat down, tilting the back of the chair against the wall.

There was a silence. Then, he said: "About pregnant women?"

"What about them?"

"Do they get funny ideas?"

"How should I know?"

"Maybe you know."

"Why?"

"I get home, and she ain't home. She comes back and says she didn't know I was coming."

"What's so funny about that?"

"Wait for the funny part. She says she's pregnant and I got to sleep on the couch. Me—after not being home so long—had to sleep on the couch."

"Maybe they're that way."

"I hear the boys tell, it's all right even in the ninth month."

"I don't know a thing about it."

"I'm trying to think when it happened. It was from before, she says, but she wasn't sure so she didn't say. It must've been an accident; I was careful. Well—it's not so bad having a kid."

"You might as well have the trimmings," I said.

Later, I said to The Yid: "We're going visiting."

"Visiting who?"

"You don't know him."

"Maybe."

"Martin Lester."

"I know about him. Ticket scalper and gambler."

"You know everything."

"Sure," he said.

"Then what do I want him for?"

"Sell him a couple of tickets for the Policemen's Ball."

"That's an idea—come on."

When we were on the street, I said: "We'll walk; it's not far; Theatre Building."

"It ain't far," The Yid said.

We walked along. The Yid asked what I really wanted Lester for. I said, for blackmail. He asked who was being blackmailed. I said that it was none of his business; would he shut up, because I did not feel like talking. He looked hurt.

We went through the arcade and into the building. The name was listed on the information board; the office was on the fifth floor. We went up in the elevator and walked down the hall to the door.

"I'll wait out here, and you go in and see if he's there. If he's not there, the girl might get wise and tip him off."

"What'll I say?"

"You said it. Say you're collecting pledges in advance for the sale of Policemen's Ball tickets."

He went in and I waited, and in a few minutes, he came back.

"He's there," he said.

"How many rooms?"

"Two."

"Watch both doors. If he lams, nab him."

I went in and told the stenographer that I was from the Stadium and wanted to talk business with Mr. Lester. She went inside and came out again and told me to go in.

Lester was sitting in front of an old roll-top desk. The office was very dirty. When I came in, he looked at me hard; then he smiled and said: "Sit down, Inspector."

"Get your hat and coat."

"What for?"

"Quit stalling. I guess I better tell you; there's a lot of rackets you're in."

He smiled; his front teeth showing gold inlays.

"Want you for the Tinevelli racket. I got a warrant. Want to read it?"

"No, no, Inspector. It's all right. I take your word for it. Can I call my lawyer?"

"Sure."

He called his lawyer and explained that he had been arrested. Would he please come with bail.

"Make it heavy," I said.

He smiled again and said into the telephone: "Better make it heavy."

We went along the corridor, The Yid following. Lester had flat feet and he sounded like a seal flopping down the hall. He smiled all the way, in the taxi-cab and in the station-house while we were booking him.

"You stay down here," I said to The Yid, and went upstairs, Lester flopping in front of me.

We went into the office. I pulled a chair in front of the desk and told him to sit down. He sat down. The stage was set; I sat down.

"You got nothing on me," he said.

I did not answer him, and he smiled, leaned back, and did not speak for a while.

"What are you waiting for?" he finally said.

"For you."

"I'll talk when I see my lawyer."

"Let's wait for him."

We sat there, and I looked directly at him, until he hung his head, closed his eyes, and made believe that he was dozing. It was that way for a pretty long time. The Yid disturbed it.

"That guy's Shyster is here."

"Fast work, that boy's fast," I said.

Lester gave us his gold toothed smile.

"What's he want?"

"Bail."

"Go out and tell him I got a man downtown on this bird's fingerprints. I guess there's a couple of gambling charges; remember a five-day sentence. Maybe it's a fourth offense, who knows. And if he don't get out, throw him out."

I saw Lester become a little pale, but he kept smiling. The Yid went out.

"Now we can work," I said. "Did you know Tinevelli took the pipe?"

"What's that got to do with me?"

"Don't be a sap. There's nobody here and you're not signing a confession. I know all about it; 'Big Stem' squealed."

He laughed and said: "I didn't talk to that rat for ten years."

"Rats got a way of boring in and biting," I said.

"Maybe."

"He got it from a speakeasy owner, a dopey, too," I said and saw his eyes go a little wide at that.

"You think that'll carry any weight?"

"You're smart. I'll bet you figured it that way."

"Your bet's safe."

"Smart, damn smart; only, a dopey will always squeal."

"What's the good. They're all liars."

"That's right, they're all liars," I said.

"If squealing's in order," Lester said, "suppose you some day ask that rat, James, who plugged Stein."

I looked at him hard and said: "I knew that. Think that'll get you off?"

"Don't need it to get me off. You got nothing."

"Think you can beat it?"

"It's open and shut."

I opened the drawer in front of me and took out the Savage pistol by the barrel and slid it across the desk so that it lay in front of him. He looked surprised.

"Know that gun?"

He reached for it, put his hand on the butt, then pulled his hand away quickly. He smiled.

"Nothing doing. That's an old one," he said.

"Look at it close. See anything you know about it?"

He reached into his breast-pocket, took out a pair of spectacles, put them on and bent over the gun, looking at it closely. I slipped my gun from its shoulder-holster and rested my elbow on the desk, pointing the gun at him.

"Lester," I said softly.

He looked up and saw the gun. His skin became the color of grey clay and he tried to smile, but the face muscles refused to work. His eyes grew big behind the glasses, and his mouth started to work as though he wanted to speak, and a few drops of spit ran out of it and dripped down from his chin. I began to pity him, so I pulled the trigger, and the gun almost kicked out of my hand.

I had been aiming at his mouth, but the second when he slammed against the wall behind him and before he slid down, I saw that the bullet had caught him between the eyes. The bullet had cut the spectacles; both pieces were hanging from the ears. He hung against the wall for a second, then slid out of sight, and the wall was dripping with pinkish-gray matter and blood and matted hair.

I gave the Savage automatic on the desk a push and it went over the side of the desk. It must have hit him first, because I heard it thud and then clatter to the floor.

Then I heard them pounding up the steps. They came running in with drawn guns. Schlegel, the civilian-clerk, was with them; he had been afraid to come in alone. When they saw me, they stopped.

"I mentioned a fourth offense and he pulled a gun, so I plugged him," I said.

They went over and looked at him. I got up and went around the desk. The bullet had made a clean hole in front, but had torn the back of the head out while coming out.

Suddenly, Schlegel began to retch; he vomited on my desk.

"Get the hell out of here. Go on in the toilet," I said.

He put his hand over his mouth and went quickly towards the door. Near the door, he could no longer control himself; the vomit shot out of his nostrils and forced itself past the sides of his hands; he took his hands away and it spattered over the door frame. He went out of the room still retching.

"Somebody tell 'Pop' to come up and clean up. Mac, call up the morgue and get this stiff out of here. The rest of you get out."

They went out. I picked up the telephone.

"Give me outside."

The operator answered and I gave her the number. I heard it ring on the other side, then someone answered. Father MacLaughlin had a class. Would I leave a message? Yes. Inspector Safiotte. Spring it. Was that, spring it? Yes. Tell his wife. Whose wife? He knows. Thank you.

XVI

The news of Teeny's death crowded the killing of Stein from the front pages of the newspapers. The authorities and the church decided that he had been temporarily insane, and he was buried in holy ground. In death, and because he had paid both ways, everything was forgotten. All of Little Italy turned out for the funeral.

The large funeral went a long way to ease the sorrow that his wife felt. She was being that which every woman in her life desires to be: the center of an attraction, and that attraction a tragedy.

The funeral made me think of my father who all his life had paid weekly installments to a funeral fund, and in the end the old lady died before him and robbed him of his fancy funeral.

The news that Teeny had made was so big that my shooting Lester was given small notice. The lawyer was inclined to make trouble; but he was one of these lawyers who win city cases and lose those outside of the city—if you know what I mean—and a few words in the proper direction was enough to quiet him.

After all the activities were over and I had nothing to keep me intense, thoughts kept pushing themselves into my mind, and I knew there would have to be an end. Having him before me every day and knowing that he was there where I was burning to be—there would have to be an end.

"You stay here," I said to him. "Be back right away."

I took my hat, went down the stairs and out on the street. It was a spring day, warm and clear. I walked along thinking that, even with sunshine, you had to die and that it was not much different if it was a few years before or a few years later.

The wide avenue was crowded with traffic. I waited until the traffic-lights were my way and crossed over and went down the street to Monk's newsstand.

"Hello, Monk." I said.

"Hello, Looey, hello. How are you?"

"Fine, Monk. You got somebody to leave here? Want you to do me a favor."

"Sure. Wait a minute."

He went into the cigar-store and came out with a boy of about fourteen. We left the boy at the stand. While we walked, I said: "You're a friend of 'Big Stem James'? You used to know him?"

"The hoppy?"

"Yes."

"Sure."

"We're going looking for him. When we find him, you tell him like this—I'm not there and don't let on I'm around—tell him: you hear from the inside that he's been picked for the Stein murder; a woman looking out of a window identified him and we're hunting him."

"Sure."

"And, Monk, keep your trap closed," I said. I did not think it was necessary to say that; he could not have figured it.

We walked along until we were a block away from the ticket-agency. I told Monk to go on and I would wait for him in the cigar-store on the corner. He went shuffling along, looking as though he did not have any legs because the coat reached to the ground.

I went into the cigar-store, bought a cigar and waited. The cigar was dry, and I threw it away after a few puffs. I waited there, and in a few minutes, I saw Monk shuffling towards me. He had his dirty handkerchief in his hand and was rubbing his big nose. I went out to meet him.

"Beat it like a house on fire," he said.

"He was there?"

"I told him and he beat it."

I took out my wallet and held out a ten dollar bill to him.

"Nothing doing, I don't take nobody's money."

"You worked for it."

"Nothing doing, not off you."

"Okey—you go on. I won't forget it."

He went away down the block.

Back in the cigar-store, I went into the telephone-booth and got The Yid on the telephone.

"Get over to 'Big Stem James's' room—Glenfair Hotel, room 913—and shake yourself. He's there now and I want to see him

148

bad. Tell him to come over. He knows you, don't he? All right. And make it on the run."

I hung up and went out of the booth and bought a cigar, making sure that it was fresh. Lighting it, I went outside and walked slowly uptown, away from the station-house. Now, it was a toss-up. Whatever came of it, I would call it a finish. "Big Stem" had said they would never take him, and he would make for his store of narcotics—roll the dice, come seven or eleven or crap.

The avenue I was walking on went into a circle, which was like the hub of a wheel, because many streets emptied into it. The street running near the station-house was one of the spokes of the wheel. I thought that enough time had passed for whatever was to happen, so I turned down the street and walked towards the station-house.

I went up the stairs into the house, and everything was quiet; nobody was downstairs but the desk-sergeant. When I went towards Captain Mac's door, the sergeant said: "The Captain's upstairs, sir. Something very serious happened. Levinson got his. They're all up in the dormitory."

"Bring him down."

He called by phone and delivered my message. I stood with my hand on the high desk, supporting myself and looking at the floor.

"It's tough," the sergeant said. "He just got hitched, didn't he?"

I nodded my head. There was a silence. The Captain came down the steps and walked over to me. I took my hand off the desk and stood up straight.

"Well," he said. "Simms tell you?"

"Yes. How bad?"

"Dead as a mackerel."

I did not say anything.

"Hits you hard, don't it?" he said.

"Hits me hard."

"I know how it is."

"How'd it happen?"

"How come he went there, I don't know. Peterson called in. He's walking his beat and all of a sudden out comes a guy from the Glenfair Hotel. There's a gun in his hand and he's running on Peterson. The house-dick—Peterson knows him—comes just behind blazing away. Peterson drops the guy coming on him; got him in the belly—he always was a hell of a good shot. He kicks around a little on the sidewalk and passes out. The guy's 'Big Stem James.'

"The house-dick tells Peterson that a guy on the ninth floor got shot. The elevator-boy comes down and yells it to the house-dick just before James, all hopped up like a smoking chimney, comes burning down the stairs. He sees the dick and takes a shot at him. The dick ducks; and the rest, what happened outside, I told you. Peterson and the house-dick go back upstairs and The Yid's laying in a lot of blood, and he's dead.

"The elevator-boy is blubbering and crying. He tells them: James comes up all excited and nervous and white and runs down the hall; right after, a guy comes up and asks where the room is. The boy watches him, curious, kind-of. The man knocks and knocks again; then the door is opened, there's a couple of shots, and the man curls up and flops on his face, and James comes running with a gun in his hand. The elevator-boy slams the gates in his face and rides down and yells. That's the story. How come he went?"

"Don't know. Maybe it's this: I told him I had an idea James was mixed with the Stein killing."

"That's it, sure, that's it. That's the Jew for you."

"Shut up, Mac. What you do about telling his wife?"

"Sent a dick up."

"How's it you brought him here; coroner look at him?"

"Not yet. Knew how you felt about it. Open and shut. Didn't want to let him laying there; brought him here."

"Better get him home. I think Jews bury their dead the next day. Better arrange for an inspector's funeral. That jackass downtown will want to show off. Anyway, we want to do everything to make it easier for his wife. Better keep the dick there to run errands."

"The boys didn't like him."

"Then they'll be glad to go to the funeral."

XVII

The afternoon paper had the story and wrote of The Yid as a hero who had given his life in the service of the city. They had a picture of Beth, and I knew that it must have been stolen by a reporter; she would not have permitted it. The Commissioner had his picture on the front page. He had made the statement saying that he would see The Yid buried as befitted a hero; he had died in the performance of his duty, he had held his trust sacred, and so on, and so on.

Late in the afternoon, after they had taken the body away, an old Jew with a long grey beard stained yellow around the mouth came in and told us in the little English he knew, that since the next day was Saturday and you cannot bury during the holy day, the funeral would be Sunday morning, at eleven. While the old man talked, he kept looking at the sky through the window, and when he was finished he gave it a long look and scurried away.

The boys grumbled at the funeral being Sunday; it was their day off. I told Captain Mac to shut them up.

"You can't blame them," he said. "They didn't like him."

"I heard that before. The old man wants it, and I want it, and they got no say."

"Sure, they got no say."

"Then let them like it or make believe they like it. Anyway, tell them they'll get their pictures in the papers. Did you ever see a cop that could resist that?"

"You're looking at him."

"You should've been a boss in a Turkish-bath, not a cop."

"I don't get you."

"You think about it, Mac."

I was very drunk Friday night and Saturday; and Saturday night I could not fall asleep. A hammer kept pounding away in the back of my head. It hurt to keep my eyes open and, when I closed them, the walls of the room—walls that I could not see— would spin around, and I had to hold on to keep the bed from sliding away from under me.

I dressed and went out on the street. It was very cold again, but the cold wind felt good. The drugstore on the corner was closed, so I walked down to the avenue where I knew I could find one open. Not minding the walk because I was feeling better, I walked about a mile. Pretty soon, I saw a drug-store open and went in. The clerk was leaning over the counter, reading a book. He looked up and then down again and creased the page to mark it.

"Yes, sir?"

"Some veronal tablets."

"Sorry; not without a prescription."

"That's funny. I get them always."

"Yes, some of the privately owned stores sell it. We can't take a chance. It's a Board of Health ruling, and we can't take a chance."

"It's all right; I'm a police inspector," I said and showed him my shield.

"All the more reason why I can't sell it."

"What've you got for sleep?"

"Some effervescent triple bromides; I can sell you those."

"Some what?"

"Effervescent triple bromides."

"Let's have 'em."

He went into the back and came out with a long blue box.

"How do you take them?"

"Take two and put them in water and when they effervesce, drink it."

"Suppose two don't work?"

"Take two more. Can't hurt you."

"Thanks. How much?"

"Eighty-nine cents."

I paid him, took my package and went out. When I looked back from the doorway, he was reading his book again.

On the street, the hammering began again and I was sorry I had not taken two tablets in the store. At home, two tablets did not relieve me; they only gave me heartburn and I had to take some bicarbonate of soda; but two more put me to sleep.

I slept so well, that it was late morning when I woke up. The clock was on the dresser just opposite the foot of the bed, and when I lifted my head a little off the pillow, I saw that it was ten minutes past ten. For a few seconds I lay back; it was so comfortable and my head was quiet; then, at once, I realized what morning it was.

By telephone I got in touch with Captain MacDunn. He told me that they were waiting for me. I said for him to go ahead with the men; I would go from home.

When I arrived uptown, they were there before me. The street was crowded with people and I had to park the car on another street. I forced my way through the crowd. The neighborhood was Jewish and most of the people were Jews. Finally, I was able to get through to the big space which the police were holding open in front of the house.

The blue-coated police were drawn up in three rows: two forming a lane reaching from the door to the hearse standing alone in the center of the street—the passenger cars were parked across the street—another row closed the lane and formed a square enclosing the hearse. It was very impressive. The newspaper photographers were in the cleared space beyond the police.

Captain Mac was standing in the doorway. I went up to him.

"Plenty of time," he said. "The big-chief undertaker ain't here yet."

"How about the Commish?"

"Been here, had his picture taken and's gone back to his Sunday dinner."

Going up the stairs, I thought of the other times that I had walked up them. The door was open and I walked in. The bedroom was on the right just before you came to the parlor. The policemen who were to act as pall-bearers were standing around the bedroom door. They nodded to me and stood away; I went in.

It was dark; the shades were drawn; a candle on the window-sill opposite the door flickered up and then died low again. It kept doing that every few seconds. The Yid was on the bare floor with his feet towards the door. He was wrapped in a white shawl with blue stripes, and I recognized the Hebrew prayer-shawl. The bed had been taken apart and the parts were standing against the wall. The bed . . . "not in the bed, it wouldn't be right."

Goddam it, I hated him because I had had to do that. A white pine coffin stood upright in the corner. The room smelled of fresh cut pine and burned tallow. I could hear a few people talking in the parlor. One, a woman, was crying and talking sing-song at the same time. It sounded like a dirge.

I went out and downstairs again and stood with Captain Mac in the doorway. After a while, two men in Prince Albert coats went upstairs. We waited a while and the policeman we had set for the signal came down and told us that they were coming.

Mac gave the signal and the policemen stood at attention. There was a stir among the newspaper photographers. First the undertakers came out, then we saw the coffin; it was covered with the flag. It went past; we stood at attention. A man holding a veiled woman's arm came next; it was Pete, the cousin—the extra day had given the relatives time to come down from up-state. For a moment, I thought the woman was Beth, but closer—she was too heavy. Pete looked at me and I nodded; he shrugged his shoulders. The woman kept availing.

The pall-bearers slid the coffin into the hearse. A group of men and women came down the alleyway from the door. They came closer and I was looking at her. Her face was white and her lips drawn together in a straight line. She was not crying, only walking along and looking at the ground. When she came near me, she raised her eyes and I looked down into them; and I felt as though someone had taken a knife and slit my stomach and gutted me; I was without insides. She passed.

The photographers were banging away with their flashlights. The hearse went slowly up the street, a row of policemen on each side, the family walking directly behind. We, the police, came next and behind us were strung out "the press," the black passenger coaches, and the patrol-wagons which had brought the policemen.

"Mac," I said, "I forgot my car. Tell one of the men who knows it to go back. Here's the key. It's around the corner."

"I'll go myself."

He left me and I walked alone.

The sun was bright and was nearly overhead, and it emphasized the black in front of me. We walked slowly in the sunlight. The people on the sidewalks were quiet and the sound of the two mounted policemen in front of the hearse was loud in the quiet. The women were crying softly. It was the woman with Pete who kept wailing at the top of her voice.

We came to the synagogue. The hearse backed up against the sidewalk; and I thought that they were going to take the casket out, but they did not, only opened the doors of the hearse. The family went up the steep steps. I saw Pete stop at the door, shake his head and come down the steps again. The family went in.

Pete came over to me; I was standing near the iron fence in front of the synagogue. He leaned against the fence and put his hands into his pockets. He had no coat on.

"You didn't want to go in?" I said.

"No. When I was sixteen, I refused to go to synagogue on Yom Kippur. My father beat me and I swore that I'd never go into one again." He hesitated and then nodded at the hearse. "How silly—with that thing—vows!"

We stood together for some time watching the beggars with their iron boxes circling through the crowd. Then, he said: "May I ride with you? My mother is making me nervous with her acting—thank God for things like this to satisfy their sense of tragedy."

I put my hand on his arm and said: "I'm glad you said that."

"Why?"

"Don't know. Just feel that way."

The family came out again; a rabbi in a prayer-shawl was with them. They all stopped in front of the open hearse, and the rabbi began to chant in a loud voice. The men lent him their "amens" and the women, their tears. When he finished, he went up the steps and into the synagogue.

Pete left me and went to the curb, and, in a quiet voice, began to arrange them in the coaches. The hearse drew away and stopped down the street, waiting for the rest. As a coach filled, it would line up behind the hearse. When they were all full, they raced away.

Mac gave the order for the policemen to disband. They went away in groups; the patrol-wagons started away; the press left in their cars.

"The wagons didn't have to follow," I said. "They could've gone back before."

"Make it look bigger," Mac said.

"Bigger and better," Pete said and smiled.

We got into my car, and I started and swung around the corner. We went very fast down the avenue. At the bridge, crossing the river, we overtook the rest of them. The rest of the way, we were in a cloud of dust.

We lined up on the paved roadway inside the cemetery and before an arch leading into one of the plots. Several old Jews had come up quickly and were talking fast in their own language, one trying to shout louder than the other.

"Who're they?" I asked Pete.

"Professional prayers, presumably holy men."

"What're they hollering about?"

"They're bargaining for price."

We walked up to the group. At the sight of Captain Mac's uniform they quieted a little. Pete counted the men present in our group, then told off three of the old men.

"Guess there has to be a certain amount," Mac said.

The hearse was opened. The cemetery men pulled the casket out. A little fat man, one of the relatives, insisted on taking the front end. He was so short that the casket tilted. When one of the cemetery men made as if to take it from him, he refused to give his place up. They passed under the arch and waited beyond it.

"Beth," Pete said.

A young woman had her under the arm, but she hung back, shaking her head and biting her lips.

"What do you mean? You've got to come," Pete said sharply.

She hung her head and passed slowly under the arch and the rest followed her.

The casket going in front, we walked among the tombstones to the grave. The men lowered the casket on to the small wooden trestle. An old man stationed himself on the far side, like a tradesman behind a counter. Beth was led to the coffin; tears

156

now were running down her face. The man mumbled something, reached across the coffin and with a knife tore a rent in her coat. She backed away.

Then everything went rapidly. The cemetery men, in their dirty overalls removed the flag, picked up the coffin, slung straps under it and lowered it into the grave. The old man, who had cut the coat, jumped down into the grave. He landed on the coffin with a thud. The men began to pray as he scooped some dirt down on the coffin, and then he bent out of sight. I learned later that he was unscrewing the lid. The cries of the women grew louder. The man came out of the grave and the grave-digger took up a shovel of sand and offered it to Beth and she backed further away from the grave. He shrugged and tossed it down into the open hole; and it fell with a rattle on the wooden coffin. The little fat man grabbed another shovel and helped cover the box. It was covered in record time and the crying died away. We all turned from the grave.

On the road again, I asked Pete: "How are you going hack?"

"Since the comedy is over, I'll go back with them."

"Is Mrs. Levinson going home—up-state?"

"No. She's staying. They fussed a little. She's better off here."

"What's she going to do?"

"Don't know. She's sunk if she goes with this bunch. She'll be sunk like I'm sunk."

"Why don't you break away?"

"I don't know what I want myself."

"What do you do?"

"Nothing."

"Nothing?"

"Just that."

XVIII

Spring had come, and there was a freshness in the air as though everything had been in hiding and was, at last, coming out into the open; nothing any more to be afraid of; no more cold or snow or slush. On one side was that and on the other, seeing her face always before me, the days dragged themselves past. She was every place . . . in the office on the papers, on the walls; in the open, mixed with the springtime.

I went in the afternoon, but she was not home. In the evening, when I called, she was there. Her face was very white when she saw me at the door, and, without saying a word, she turned around and walked down the hallway. I went in and closed the door behind me and followed her. She sat down in the chair near the window, turning her head so that she looked through the glass. I sat down.

"How are you?" I said.

"Why did you come?"

"I had to know—to know how you are."

"I'm all right."

"That's good. I'm glad. What are you going to do?"

"I haven't decided yet. The first few months, nothing—I'm pregnant."

"I know; he told me. You should decide."

"After I get over the first months, I'll work. I'm sick."

"You shouldn't."

"I want to—I want to be occupied. When I show, I'll stop. I have enough."

"I know—the insurance. I didn't mean that. You know why I came."

"I'm not stupid."

"Maybe you don't know."

"I do."

"How about it?"

"No."

"I mean marry."

She did not answer right away; then, "No."

"I'll make it nice for you. Maybe, because I insulted you, you don't believe me?"

"You actually think you love me."

"Sure, I do."

"You couldn't, Buck. I wouldn't chance it."

"And you talked about love," I said. "If you loved me, you wouldn't act like that."

"Because of that I won't marry. I do, I do—it's sunk so far into me, I can't even say it; and I won't let you dirty it."

"You're wrong. I'll make it nice for you."

"I couldn't, really, I couldn't."

"Is that guy still in the way?"

"Don't."

"He was in the way."

"Please. I think I'll go crazy thinking about it. It was in my thoughts, but I didn't want it that way. God knows, I didn't want it that way."

"What's the difference; he was in the way?"

"There, Buck, can't you see yourself why I'm afraid to marry you?"

"Why should I feel sorry?"

"He didn't do anything wrong. We were just unfortunate."

"All right, he didn't do anything wrong, but wasn't he in your way? Didn't you have to sleep with him?"

"I didn't till I was sure."

"Sure?"

"The baby was there."

"What's the difference?"

"I didn't want you to know; I didn't want you to feel obligated—it's yours."

There was a silence; then I said: "Well, maybe—how do you know?"

"Don't humiliate me by making me tell you how I know."

Well, I thought, maybe. It did not make any difference; I did not feel anything towards it.

I looked at her sitting there, and I thought of the other times, and I was excited.

"It don't make any difference, his or mine," I said. "I want to get married to you."

"You don't believe me?" she asked.

"I guess so. How about it?"

"No, Buck."

"All right," I said. I was angry and I was not going to beg.

"Don't."

I got up and so did she, and I saw her start to breathe heavily, and when I turned to go out, she fell on the floor. I picked her up and put her on the couch and rubbed her temples. She did not come out of it, so I went into the kitchen and got a glass of water and wet her forehead and tried to force some between her lips. The water washed some of the powder off her face and the part which was wet was duskier than the rest. She lay so still; I did not think she was breathing—just like a woman: they never know what they want. I slapped her face, putting force behind the slap. Where I had hit her, the blood started to come in. She moved and opened her eyes.

"You're going to stop being foolish," I said.

She began to cry. I let her cry for a while; then, "I can't fight the two of us," she said.

"Fight? You don't have to fight; I'm going to make it nice for you."

She did not say anything.

"It's settled," I said. "When?"

"But it's only a month."

"Thirty days or a year, what's the difference to him—you're beginning again."

"We ought to be decent about it. What will they say?"

"Who's they?"

"Everybody."

"Who's everybody?"

"Oh, everybody. You're not a nothing. There would be talk."

"That's nothing to me. If they don't like it—"

"It won't be nice for me."

"We don't have to advertise it. When they find out they wouldn't know who you are. We'll go up here to this county-clerk."

"I hope it's all right."

"I guess we can get rid of this junk in a week."

I bent over her; she was on the couch.

"I want a kiss."

I pushed my arms under her and kissed her. While I was kissing her, I pressed myself hard against her. She pushed me away and said, "Next week."

I smiled and rubbed her chin with my knuckles.

"And, Buck," she said. "I know it sounds foolish, after we— after all this." . . . She hesitated.

"Yes?"

"I want to be married by a rabbi."

"Sure, anything, Beth."

Friday morning I had my breakfast, put on my coat and stood in the kitchen doorway. Myra was drying the dishes. I said: "Forgot to tell you, I'm getting married today."

She stopped wiping the plate and stood still, the towel in one hand and the plate in the other; then she slowly put them down and slowly wiped her hands on the apron.

"You don't have to be afraid about the job," I said. "You can still come and clean up."

Rocking back a little on her heels, she suddenly began to laugh.

"What's funny about me getting married?"

She shook her head slowly several times from side to side and kept laughing. Then she said, "Clean up," and laughed again with her lips closed tight.

"Laugh and be damned," I said and went out slamming the door.

I never saw her again.

In the afternoon we went for the license, and it was late when we were finished swearing that we had never had a venereal disease. The paper was in my pocket—I had placed after the word "occupation": policeman. We walked down the steps and across the small park in front of the County-Hall. The days were becoming longer; it was five o'clock, and it was still light. There was some grass on the lawn, and the bushes and the trees were showing green buds. The air smelled of fresh earth.

She put her arm through mine and we passed through the stone gateway to the walk.

"Now, how d'you find a rabbi?" I said.

"There's one around the corner from . . . I'm hungry; I want to eat first."

We walked over the car-tracks to the other side of the street and went into a restaurant and had something to eat. Out on the sidewalk again, we walked to where I had the car parked and got in.

I started the car and drove down the street under the elevated until I came to the park. In the park where it was quiet, I said: "In the end, you're where you belong."

She put her hand on my hand, which was on the wheel.

The sun was going down and it began to darken, and it was dusk when we walked up the steep stoop of the rabbi's house. It was an English style house; one of a row of the same kind, with a high stone stoop and a downstairs entrance under the steps. We had stopped for a minute to decide whether to ring upstairs or downstairs; since the small glass sign was in the upper window, we went up and rang the bell. There were no lights in the house and, for a moment, we thought there was nobody at home.

"Maybe he's in synagogue," Beth said. "It's nearly Sabbath. Maybe we're too late."

"Ring again."

Just as she was going to ring, we heard the rattle of the iron grille-door under the stoop. I leaned over the railing and saw a woman. She looked up and said something that I did not understand. Beth leaned over and spoke to her in Yiddish. The woman went back and in a few minutes came to the upper door. She had a candlestick in her hand. We walked behind her, and she ushered us into a long, narrow parlor. The only light came from her candle and a candlestick with seven candles standing on a small table at the end of the room. It was more like a funeral than a wedding.

The woman went out.

"Why don't they put on the lights?" I asked Beth.

"I suppose because it's nearly Sabbath. Maybe we are too late. You can't marry on the Sabbath."

"Think a rabbi is going to pass up a piece of change?"

"Buck!"

The rabbi came in. He was tall and wore a small, pointed beard. His face was round and pleasant looking.

"Want to get married?" he said in English, and smiled.

"Yes," I said.

"It will take a few minutes for me to get together a 'minion.'"

I said: "That's all right."

"I have three sons," he said. "I can get the rest from the neighbors."

"It's all right," I said.

"Your license, please."

I took the license out of my pocket and gave it to him. He looked at it and said: "I won't keep you long. We must hurry; it will soon be dark."

"That's all right," I said.

He went out, and I said to Beth: "What's a 'minion'?"

"Ten men. There must be that number at every sacred ceremony."

A boy of about eight years came in and stood silently watching us.

"Come here, son," I said.

He came over to me and I noticed his eyes: they were large and dark, and in the dim light looked as though they were all pupil. He was a pretty child with his dark, curly hair and oval face, looking at us under his brows as though he did not have to grow and live to know; all the knowing was there.

"What's your name?" I said.

"Uriel."

"What a beautiful name," Beth said.

The boy looked at her and said: "What's 'beautiful'?" He said the long word with difficulty, but it was clear. His voice was very sweet.

Beth said: "He has a nice voice."

"I sing in a 'chore'," the boy said.

"Is he part of the 'minion'?" I asked her.

"No," she said with a smile. "He's too young."

We heard several people coming up the steps. The rabbi came in with the required number of men and his wife.

"Did I keep you waiting?" he said.

"Not at all," Beth said.

"Uriel, go downstairs."

"Please let him stay," Beth said.

"Will you step this way?"

Beth and I got up. All eyes were on us. We walked after the rabbi to the end of the room and he lifted the candlestick and put it on a small table under a canopy. There was a bottle of wine, a saucer and a glass on the table. Beth walked under the canopy and I followed her. The boy, Uriel, had followed us and stood at my side and just a little in front of me, looking at me. I saw the candlestick reflected in his eyes.

The rabbi began the ceremony, and I watched the boy and wondered why he never smiled.

The walls were covered with some kind of dark material shot through with gold; and the gold reflected the flickerings of the candles.

"The ring, please?"

I gave it to him and he gave it back.

"On the index-finger. Hold it and repeat after me."

I repeated words that did not mean anything to me.

The rabbi poured a glass of wine from the bottle; he chanted a short time, then handed the glass to me.

"Drink, please."

I took a sip; it was very sweet and thick. The glass was given to Beth then, and she drank. The rabbi poured the rest of the wine into the saucer and bent and put the glass at my feet. He got up and smiled.

"Step on it," Beth said.

I brought my heel down hard on it; it shattered. There was a murmur among the men watching.

Beth and I kissed, and the "minion" went out without saying anything—they had come and they were gone. The rabbi shook hands with us; his wife was sweeping up the broken glass.

I paid the rabbi and we turned to go out.

"Good-night, Uriel," Beth said.

I put my hand on his head and shook it and said, "Night, son."

The rabbi smiled and said: "Your license. Will you sign, please? I almost forgot it in my hurry. It is very late." He turned to the woman and spoke to her in Jewish. She went out and downstairs and, while we were signing, she came back with two men.

"My sons," the rabbi said.

I nodded. They did not smile. One looked at Beth and kept his eyes on her, even while he was signing. She became conscious of it and turned sideways to him, and, when the license was finished and in my pocket, took my arm. We went out.

BOOK THREE

XIX

The summer came and the hot days; days that did not have the redemption of being dry. The wetness was like a large, invisible vapor that pressed down on the body until it was as though there was no longer any air to breathe. It kept that way for periods of a week or more; then would come the cool rains and the cooling winds out of the ocean; and it was like coming out of a nightmare and finding that it was a dream.

Beth was big with her child. I saw how the heat was with her and suggested that she go and stay at the beach. She refused. It would not be convenient. She liked home comforts; and it was cool in the house, with the park just across the street.

In the evenings, we would walk in the park. It had to be night before she would go out; only when it was cool and she could wear her coat, did we go out during the daylight. They were pleasant evenings.

Several times, I had to plead night-duty and sleep it off in a hotel. Once, there was a woman, and, seeing Beth the next day, with her swollen stomach, I was ashamed and knew it was only because I had been drunk; and I knew that she still held me.

After that, we walked more often and the night-duty became less. We would come home and not talk much; and always for her a bath before going to bed. I would be on my side of the bed, listening to her bathing, and trying to keep away from her side so that the sheets would be cool for her. She would come in, smelling of talcum, say good night, turn around a little and fall asleep. She fell asleep very easily.

We never talked about the coming thing. When she had first gone to a doctor and I had asked her who it was, she had told me that it was a woman doctor; she was ashamed before a man. But when she was big, and she switched to a man doctor, and I asked her why, she said that the doctor was a distant relative of her aunt.

"I thought she was sore at you?" I asked.

"When I wrote her about the baby," she answered. "She's not half bad," she said.

I said for her to suit herself.

Finally, the summer was gone and there were the cool days of autumn. The opening of the theatres and night-clubs and the return of the crooks, gamblers and whores kept me downtown more than during the summer. To those who do not know, this seems strange; most of the crooks and women left the city during the summer and followed the crowds to the summer resorts and the racetracks. They came back in the fall, and we were kept busy making them come into line again.

That day was one of the hot days that come in the cool of autumn; and I did not want to go very far for my lunch. There was a lunch-wagon near the station-house; I went in and walked down to the end, in order to be as far away from the hot grill as possible. It was not very busy here in the wagon.

The proprietor was leaning over the counter and talking to a man. I sat down on the end stool and put my hat on the stool next to me; the man, whom the proprietor was talking to, sat next. I gave my order to the proprietor and he relayed it to one of the counter-men.

"Yes," he said to the man, "he fell asleep in my arms. His wife said, 'He's dead'; and I thought to myself only I didn't say it, because she wouldn't understand—if she only knew, if only he had known. There is no death. I used to meet him on the steps and say: 'Look out of the window, look at the trees, bare now, like death; but they're not dead.' And he'd say: 'All I know is that I can still urinate today; tomorrow . . . ' I wanted to loan him some books on Christian Science, but he wouldn't take them. If he only knew."

My order interrupted him. He put it in front of me. I began to eat, and he went back to the man.

"If they only knew: there is no power but God's. My little boy—he's only four—he knows that. If he pulls a drawer and it's too much for his little strength, he says: 'There is no power but God's; out evil,' and he gives the drawer a big pull and it comes out."

"I felt that way," the man on the stool said. "I felt that way when my pup died. I tried every darn thing. He had distemper, and I fooled with every medicine and had a veterinarian, but he died. If I didn't do everything, I wouldn't have felt so bad. I thought it was my fault. It was like having your hands tied behind your back. I realized then that even a pup's life was outside of my reach. Maybe if I'd asked instead of being so smart with medicine, he wouldn't have died. He was a good pup. As sick as he was, whenever I'd open the store—I had him in back of the store—his eyes pasted together and hardly able to stand up, he'd come out, his tail wagging. Jesus Christ, I liked him. You wouldn't believe it; I cried over it."

"I believe you," the proprietor said. "Maybe it was meant as a lesson when there is a greater need. Have you any children? No? You will have. No—you're not too old. You will have. They're God. Remember that, they're God. You watch, the first few minutes of the child's life, it looks just like you, the exact double, every feature. No, it's not the imagination of your desires; it's God."

The man got up and said: "Well, so-long, Bradey. See you some more tomorrow."

When the man had got up, he had pushed my hat off the stool. He bent and picked it up. I made believe I had not noticed, so that he would not have to apologize. He put the hat back on the stool and went down the car and out.

A little while later, I paid for my food and left.

XX

The next day was Sunday, and it was cool again. I lay in bed listening to Beth taking the screens out of and shutting the windows. She came into the room and I saw that she was trying not to make any noise; I sat up.

"Awake, Buck?"

"No, I'm sitting in my sleep."

She laughed and let up the window-blind, and the sunlight came into the room.

"I hate it dark," she said.

"Can't sleep if it isn't pitch dark."

"I know, but I hate it dark. Come on, get up. What do you want for breakfast?"

"Anything."

"I'll never be able to pin you down to something definite. Don't you like anything in particular? I'll go down and get it."

"No. Don't go down. Make it eggs and some coffee."

"Is that all?"

"When'll you have dinner?"

"Any time you want—one or two."

"Coffee and eggs. I want to be hungry for dinner. One meal in a week I want to take my time and enjoy."

I shaved and dressed. We had our breakfast together. While she washed and dried the dishes, I sat in the parlor and read the paper. When she finished, she came in.

I said: "What'll we do today? How about a ride before dinner?"

"Have to clean up the house. You go ahead, Buck. You're only in the way."

"Let me get that nigger. Why don't you let the nigger clean up for you? Want to save money for me?"

"It isn't that. I feel it's mine—my job."

"Leave it for once. Nobody comes to us anyway," I said.

"Don't be silly. Of course you can't see it, but it is dirty even for ourselves. It won't take me long. You go ahead. As soon as I'm finished, I'll have to start making dinner. Go ahead."

"I'll be back," I said.

"Come back about one o'clock."

I went down in the elevator. The boy showed me his gold teeth in a wide smile.

"Pretty soon, Boss—pretty soon?"

I said, "Yes."

"Hope it's a boy, nice big boy."

"Yes," I said. I supposed it was the proper thing to wish for a boy.

Outside on the street, I did not know where to go, so like the lion-trainer who pets cats on his day off, I got the car and went downtown to the stationhouse.

I saw Mac—I don't think I ever came in and did not find him. We played cards and had a few drinks. It was half-past twelve when I stopped playing. He protested.

"I have to get home," I said.

"What for? Let's get drunk. I feel like getting drunk."

"You're drunk now."

"Not drunk, but I'm going to get drunk."

"You get drunk. I have to get home; promised her I'd get home."

"A 'her'; all the time it's a lousy 'her' that interferes with a man's pleasure."

"Cut it out. I'm married."

He looked at me a few seconds; then he said: "Well, I'm a son-of-a-bitch!"

"You are."

"Sure, I am; I'm a . . ."

"All right, all right, didn't I say you are?"

"Sure I . . ."

"Well, you are, and a lousy one."

"Sure, I am—but I'd like to see the 'she' that can keep you in one bed."

"We don't talk about it, see?"

"Sure. Jesus Christ—like that, just like that!"

I picked up my hat and coat and walked to the door.

"Don't go shouting, you snotty Scotchman," I said and slammed the door.

Why I was so angry all the way home, I do not know. I supposed it was mostly about myself; Mac had not said anything that was offensive. The offense was in myself.

Beth was in the kitchen when I walked in. She looked at me once and seeing my face flushed from drink, turned her back to me and went on with her cooking, without saying a word. I knew that the silence was on between us. When she was angry, she spoke only when it was necessary. I hated it.

And a whole day to go through with, I thought. I wanted to say to her to forget it, but I could not, because I had been hating myself for her.

We ate in silence. The meal finished, I went into the parlor and back to my paper, reading until the lines swam together. I lay down on the sofa and fell asleep. When I woke up, it was pretty late. Beth was sitting in the armchair near the window and reading a book. I went into the bathroom and washed my face with cold water and went back into the parlor and said: "Want to see a movie?"

She got up, went to the closet and got her coat and hat. I put on mine and we went out and down in the elevator. While we were walking, I tried to make my face pleasant, so nobody would know there was anything between us, and by the time we came to the theatre, my face muscles hurt. The darkness and quiet in the theatre were good. I was sorry when it was over and we had to go out.

It was dark but I felt uncomfortable walking separate with a pregnant woman. At last, we came to the house. Beth stopped near the entrance, leaned against the wall and looked out at the park.

"Going upstairs?" I said.

She did not answer.

"Stop being a damn fool and come on up," I said.

Again she did not say anything.

"All right. Me, I'm going up," I said and left her standing there and went upstairs.

By the time I had my hat and coat off, she rang the bell. I opened the door and let her in, and I almost laughed: a woman big with a child trying to look dignified.

She went into the bedroom and I went into the kitchen and made some coffee. While I was drinking it, I heard her go into the bathroom and heard the water rush into the bathtub. When I went into the bedroom, her clothes were lying on the chair and I heard her washing in the tub. I undressed, put out the light, and lay down in the dark.

Pretty soon, she came out of the bathroom and came into the bed. She moved around as if she was uncomfortable; then, in a little while, was asleep. Her foot was against mine; it was warm and moist from the bath.

I could not sleep, so I lay there with my eyes open, trying to think of some way to fall asleep. The foot that was against mine jerked away and I heard her moan in her sleep. The moan continued and became a sharp cry, and she was up. I reached up and put on the bed-light.

"What's the matter?" I asked.

"O Buck, my stomach."

"What's the matter?"

"A terrible bellyache."

"Did you take your cascara? You're supposed to."

"Yes."

"It's the meat you ate."

"I don't know."

"Sure it's the meat you ate. Better take an enema. Go ahead, take an enema. You'll feel better."

She got out of bed turning sideways, under the impression I would not see her bulging stomach. I turned my eyes away and heard her go to the drawer (she kept the enema-bag in the dresser-drawer), and I then she went into the bathroom. A few minutes later, I got off the bed and knocked on the door.

"Don't come in. Please, don't come in," she said.

"Don't forget the soap and the high enema tube," I said.

"I'm using it."

I went back to bed. When she came out, I saw that I he enema had not helped her.

"It's just as bad," she said.

"Lay down and try to rest. Lay quiet. Here, curl up, press your knees up. That'll relieve you."

She lay as I had told her. I put out the light. In a few seconds she began to moan and move her body.

"It's no use; it's getting worse."

I put on the light.

"Did you get anything out?" I asked.

"Yes."

"Maybe it's the other thing."

"I'm not due for three weeks."

"What's the pain like? Does it come and go?"

"It's steady."

"It has to come and go?"

"Yes."

"Maybe it's the meat?"

"I don't know, I don't know. It's terrible."

She got off the bed and went into the bathroom. Her face was white when she came out. I got out of bed and helped her. She was almost doubled over with pain. As we passed the dresser, she put her hands, palms down, on it and rested her weight on her arms.

"Let me stand here. I feel better standing up," she said.

I stood watching her standing there, weaving from side to side. Suddenly there was the spatter of water on the floor.

"What's that?" I said. "What's that?"

"I don't know."

"Maybe it's the other. Maybe it's your water broke. I'd better call the doctor."

"Let's wait. I don't want to be a false alarm."

We waited but it did not get any better.

"Is it still steady?"

"Yes."

"I guess I better call him."

"All right. I can't stand it any longer. He'll have to give me something."

I called the doctor by telephone. Yes, he'd be right over. About half an hour. Maybe less. He was dressed, and it would not take long; it was not far. Good-bye.

I went back into the bedroom.

"Lay down, Beth. You'll feel better."

She lay down and kept rolling from side to side, moaning a little under her breath. Her chin quivered a little, then snapped together, teeth hitting teeth when the pain became worse.

"Try to lay still. Rolling around don't help it."

"I can't. It's terrible. He'll have to give me something."

That was the way it was when the doctor came. I let him in when he rang the bell. He was young—it was the first time that I had seen him. We went into the bedroom.

"What is it?" he asked.

"I don't know. Please give me something."

"Here, twist over. Lie crosswise, this way. Let your feet hang over the bed."

He pulled the cover over her, stooped over and put his hand under the cover; she winced. He straightened up.

"It's the goods all right," he said.

"That's what I thought," I said. "I guess it was her water broke."

"Can't tell. Where's the hospital?"

"It's down the street a ways."

"We'll go in my car," he said.

"Get my clothes, Buck," Beth said.

"You don't need any clothes," the doctor said. "Just slip on a pair of shoes and a coat."

He went into the bathroom. I brought her shoes and stockings and bent down.

"I'll put them on," she said and stooped over and then straightened up quickly again.

"I can't," she said.

I put on her stockings and shoes, put my arm under hers and helped her off the bed. The doctor came out of the bathroom, wiping his hands on a towel. I put her coat around her over her arms.

"Has she a heavy coat? Better put on a winter coat," the doctor said.

I changed the coats. Beth put both her hands on my arm and walked with me towards the door. She squeezed hard.

"Have you nightgowns?" the doctor asked.

"I forgot," Beth said.

"Better put some baby clothes with them," the doctor said.

"They won't let you use them. They use their own," Beth said.

I went back and got two nightgowns out of the dresser and carried them in my hand.

"Why didn't you take the Boston-bag," she said when she saw me carrying them.

"Don't need it. I can bring some more tomorrow."

We went out. I pressed the elevator bell and heard it ring downstairs. While we waited, Beth held on to my arm, squeezing it.

"Buck, you don't know Doctor Shuster," she said. "This is my husband," to the doctor.

"How d'you do, Inspector."

I nodded my head and did not say anything, but pressed the bell again. The sound of the gate slamming came up to us and the elevator started up. When the Negro opened the door and saw us, his eyes opened wide. We got in and rode down. The elevator-boy kept rolling his eyes around and looking at Beth. The elevator stopped and the boy opened the gate. We got out and went through the lobby to the street.

It was cool outside and Beth pulled the coat around her, letting go my arm to do it. We took her under the arms and helped her into the car. I went in the back seat of the car with her. We started and rode down the street.

On the way down, we went over a stretch of cobbled pavement and the doctor put on a burst of speed. We bumped a lot.

"Can't you go slower?" Beth said.

"You're better off. I want to bounce you."

"Sure, you're better off," I said.

"I'll never live through it."

The doctor laughed and said: "You'll laugh at yourself."

"I tell you it's terrible. I'll never live through it."

I said: "Don't be foolish. It'll be over in no time."

"She'll scream yet," Doctor Shuster said. "This is nothing. When you'll be screaming it'll be over soon."

"If it gets worse, I'll die."

"You won't die, but you'll scream plenty."

"That's the place. There, with the lights," Beth said.

We stopped in front of the house with the lights.

The sanitarium was a two story house which had been a private dwelling and had been fixed over into a small maternity hospital. A canopy went from the door to the curb. We got out and went under the canopy to the door and I rang the bell. In a few seconds, a nurse opened the door. She saw us and took Beth under the arm and did not say a word, and we went up a few steps and into the hall. There was a stairway going to the upstairs. Under the stairway was the registration desk. A green shaded light was on it. The nurse sat Beth in a chair and sat down in front of the desk.

"Your name?"

Beth answered her. Husband's name? Doctor's name? All this in a low tone and Beth moving around in pain.

"I feel terrible. I think I'm going to vomit," she said.

The nurse got up and led Beth into the bathroom. We heard her retching. They came out, and the nurse took her into another room in the back of the house. The nurse came out in a minute.

"Did you bring a bathrobe or kimono?"

"No. I brought a nightgown."

"I'll get her one," the nurse said and went to the front of the house.

I went into the room into which she had led Beth. She was on the bed.

"Buck, I can't stand it."

"You'll have to. Don't be foolish."

"I'm going to die. I'll die."

The nurse came in and smiled and said: "They all say that. Sit up and let's get this thing around you. You'll feel better sitting up. You've got a long wait."

"Isn't it going to stop soon?"

"How often are you getting pain?"

"All the time."

The nurse smiled. "Come out in the hall and sit down. You'll feel better sitting up. And try your damnedest to make it real pain. This way, it will be a long time."

"I don't want it to get worse."

"The worse it will get, the sooner it'll be over," the nurse said.

We were in the hall and the doctor heard the nurse and said: "She'll scream plenty."

"You don't believe me. None of you believe me. Just because I don't scream, none of you believe me. It's terrible—you don't know how it is. None of you know how it is."

"I have two children," the nurse said.

"I'll die anyway," Beth said but kept quiet after that.

We sat a while. Then Doctor Shuster said: "Let's go out and sit in the car. It's uncomfortable here."

We went out and got into the car. We talked. How had it come—when? Not long, I said. We were in a movie the afternoon. We had seen "Our Blushing Brides." He had seen it, he said. The rewards of sin and the triumph of virtue—it was enough to make even a harlot weep. Pause. Yes, he went on, she had a long time before her. Probably morning. This was his first delivery in a hospital. His patients who could afford sanitariums never had any kids, they usually gave birth to gastric neoplasms; and the ones that had kids couldn't afford sanitariums— dropped them at home. Sanitariums were better in case of an emergency. Nice, very nice little place. We sat in silence a while. He talked again. He had ambitions. Not so much about money, but he wanted to do a lot. Did I ever hear of Lessamine? No? Only sold in drugstores and in one ounce containers. At least, that he would leave to the laity. At best, it was a poor bid for immortality, but he was young. Yes, I said, he was young. Lots of time, plenty of time. He asked, did I ever hear the one about the woman who, after she gave birth, looked up from the table and saw the doctor with the needle and catgut in his hand. No? He told it. Then I told the one about the two wrestlers who got tangled up. Then, he had his turn and I had mine again.

After a while, we went back in, and the doctor examined Beth. He shook his head. I said a few words to her and she told me again that she would never be able to stand it. We went out again. This time, we sat and dozed until the light began to come up. It came up behind the trees in the park and the trees stood out dark against it.

"Let's walk a little," Doctor Shuster said.

We got out and walked in the park. The sun was up when we came back.

"I'll go in and see her again and if there's nothing, I've got to go and see a few patients. I'll call in every ten minutes. If anything happens, then I can be down fast."

Beth was still in the hall when we came in. The doctor took her into the room in the back. He came out and said: "Nothing yet. I'll phone in. You'd better go in. She wants to lie down."

I went into the room. Beth was on the bed, moving in pain.

"That won't help," I said. "Why don't you lay still?"

"I can't. Just because I don't scream, you don't believe it hurts."

"Sure, I believe you," I said.

She lay on the bed and moved around, moaning a little in a low voice. I sat down and put my elbow on my knee and my head on my hand. I was tired and began to drowse. Beth shook me and said: "Don't sleep, Buck, please don't sleep."

That was repeated several times. I began to become a little angry. I could not see how my not sleeping could help her. Pretty soon, a nurse carrying a breakfast tray walked past the door.

A strange nurse came in. She was small and dark and spoke with a Spanish accent and very rapidly. Would I please go out? I went out and stood in the hall. In a few minutes the nurse came out and I went back in.

"She's terrible," Beth said. "She hurt me terribly."

"I guess she knows her business," I said and sat down.

The doctor came in.

"The delivery-nurse just told me. Want to go for breakfast, Inspector?" he said.

"Hell, yes. I need some coffee bad. We'll be back, Beth."

Her answer was a moan.

Walking down the avenue, I said: "How do you think she is? How long do you think it will be?"

"Not till tonight. I'm almost sure, not till tonight. I'll examine her again when we get back and if there's no sign, I'll have to leave again."

We came to a small restaurant and went in and had breakfast, and on the way back to the hospital spoke of it again. Yes, about eight o'clock at night, he figured. No, nothing could be done about it. If she would only try and bring it down. She was not trying hard enough. She was trying not to cause herself pain when pain was necessary. What she was having now was nothing compared to what she would have. She would scream plenty.

The door to the sanitarium was open and we walked in. The doctor was in front of me and suddenly he started to run down the hall and I saw what it was: the nurse was leading Beth into the delivery-room at the end of the hall. The nurse was smiling and nodding her head to the doctor. Beth was crouched over in pain. The three of them went into the delivery-room. I opened the door and walked in after them. They were strapping Beth's feet to the two posts on the delivery-table.

"You'll have to stay outside," the nurse said.

"Better stay outside, Inspector. As tough as they are, I've seen them on the floor and had to let them lie till I was through. Here, take my hat and coat out."

Taking his hat and coat, I went out into the hall and put them on a chair. I had not been wearing a coat, only a hat.

The nickeled sterilizer near the delivery-room door was hot and I moved down the hallway where it was cool.

There was a small glass window, more like a peephole, in the door of the delivery-room. I could see the doctor's face through it. He bent low and then I saw him nearing the door. It swung open and the doctor came out wearing a white apron and rubber gloves.

"In a half-hour at the most," he said and ducked back into the room.

Through the door, I could hear their voices. I moved a little nearer.

"I never wear rubber gloves," the doctor said.

"It's a rule of the house," the nurse said.

"I'm wearing them. Nothing ever did happen."

"Can't I rest, can't I put my legs down so I can rest. It hurts me, keeping my legs like this," Beth said.

"Now stop that. You have to help, not try to stop us. Every time you get a pain, squeeze. The more you squeeze, the sooner you'll get your feet down."

"I can't—Oh!!!"

"Squeeze," the nurse said. "Here, hold on to me. Pull . . ."

Now walk up and down, up and down the narrow hall and past the nickeled sterilizer in which I saw myself reflected out of proportion like in a defective mirror, past the dumbwaiter door, the bathroom door and the desk and back again towards the delivery-room, the doctor's face larger as I came nearer, and then over again. And squeeze. Now, squeeze and pace and squeeze again.

"Try, Beth," the doctor said.

"I am, you don't know how I am."

"All right. Now, squeeze . . ."

"Can't I take my feet down? Only for a few minutes. Please, only for a few minutes."

"For God's sake, squeeze now—squeeze now!"

I stood still, looking at the door. The doctor's head bent out of sight.

"All right, nurse, five minutes. Now, ten more."

The smell of ether. There was a silence and then a shriek and silence again. Then the nurse said: "God, that was fast work. That was fast."

"That's not the first time I've had them come with the umbilical around the neck."

"Baby, that was fast."

The doctor's head appeared again in the small window. He held something up to the light and looked at it closely.

"All there," he said.

"Why doesn't she cry?" Beth said.

There was a slap, slap, and then a baby's cry.

"Satisfied?" the doctor said. "How'd you know it was a girl?"

"I knew."

"Doctor, doctor," the nurse said loudly.

He bent suddenly. The nurse came to the door and shouted: "Miss Train, Miss Lavel, Miss Train, hurry, some help, please. Hurry up!"

The two nurses ran from the rooms and went towards her.

"Miss Train, catgut in a hurry."

One went to a closet, the other went with the delivery-nurse into the room. The nurse at the closet took something out and followed them.

I stood holding on to the dumbwaiter door-catch, feeling the heat start up from my feet and go up to my head. Perspiration on my wrists made my shirt cuffs cling to them. My eyelids felt hot and perspiring.

They were in there for a little while. I took my handkerchief out of my pocket and wiped my wrists and face. One nurse came out and went back to the front of the house. Doctor Shuster came to the door.

"All right, Inspector, come in."

He swung the door wide and I went in. The first thing I saw was the red. The doctor; the nurses; even the window opposite the foot of the operating table was spattered with it.

The doctor and the nurses were grouped around her. She saw me and smiled and I smiled back.

"Give her another shot of gynergyn," the doctor said. "One of you knead it. Knead it till it hardens."

The delivery-nurse inserted a hypodermic needle into Beth's leg; the muscles of the leg quivered. The nurse pulled the needle out quickly and wiped the spot with iodine. The tall nurse—Miss Lavel, I think her name was—stopped kneading and went over to the mesh basket in which the baby was. She bent over it and then turned around.

"Doctor, the umbilical is bleeding."

"What?" he said and went to the basket.

"Another piece of tape, please."

He worked rapidly with his fingers. "That will hold now," he said.

The delivery-nurse went out. Miss Lavel took her place again at kneading the stomach.

"Keep kneading till it hardens. The gynergyn will take soon," the doctor said and went out.

"I don't see why he doesn't pack her," the nurse said.

I came near the table and looked down at Beth. Her face looked tired, as though she had been doing days of labor without sleep.

"You got your shape back, didn't you, kid?" I said. I could think of nothing else to say.

She nodded and smiled. "It's a girl, Buck. You don't know how I prayed for a girl."

I looked at the child. Its face was towards me and I looked at it hard. I could not see any likeness.

"Here you are, Mister. Your turn now," the nurse said. "Come here. Put your hands under. Feel it? Dig in, man, dig in. Feel? That's got to stay hard. Go ahead. I'm going to take care of the baby."

The thing under my fingers went soft as she spoke. I dug my fingers in and kneaded. The nurse took the wire basket and went out.

"You don't have to dig so hard. You're hurting me."

"I want to hurt you. That'll have to harden."

"Please, Buck, let me rest. When are you going to let me rest?"

"When it gets hard."

My wrists ached, but it had stayed hard now for several minutes. The doctor came in and felt it.

"Okey—you go home now and get some sleep. She'll be all right now."

"Maybe we should knead some more?"

"No. Go home. You're all in."

"Go ahead, Buck. Don't go in today. Go home and sleep," Beth said.

"I guess I will," I said.

Outside, I stopped at a drug-store and called the station-house and left word that I would not be in. Then, I went home and got into the bed and slept about two hours.

When I got up, I went downstairs and walked very quickly to the sanitarium. They told me that she was sleeping quietly. I went home again.

BOOK FOUR

XXI

How the days went, I do not know, so I cannot tell it. One day went into the next one—well, like dissolving. Maybe like this: like the shifting scenes of a good dream, a dream in which the sleep is so deep that the living around the sleeper makes no mark on him.

The winter came and there was the snow, and then suddenly it was spring again and the snow was gone and it was green in the park again.

At first it was nothing, then it grew upon you; and when it was growing, until it was all there, you did not know it. When I thought of it, I imagined it like the veins of a leaf when you look through it at the sun; so many that you cannot see the in-between spaces, all veins and no more the original leaf. I found the child in my mind all the time. During the day, I would suddenly realize that I was saying over to myself the sounds she made and that I was hoping the day would be finished quickly. Perhaps it was like that with me because it was so late. Young ones—I think with them it is not so much, but when a man gets to my age and has one near him and watches it grow, the thing grows and covers him until it is himself.

Of the hot summer days, I remember only the green park, the baby's hair, dark and curly and wet with perspiration, and the salty taste of the perspiration on her forehead when I kissed her. And presently the heat was over and again it was autumn. The baby began to walk and to talk—and where you thought there was no more room, more veins spread over you and held you.

I had been working late that night and it was a few minutes past midnight when I started home. I went by subway because the car was in the repair shop getting an overhauling.

At home, I took off my coat, vest, and tie and went into the kitchen to see if there was something left for me to eat. Snapping the light on, I thought it would be better if I took the baby to the bathroom first. I always did that when I came home late.

I went into the bedroom and stooped over the crib to pick the baby up. My knee hit against the metal sliding side and it clattered. Picking up the child, her face against mine, I felt that her face was wet, sticky wet and smelled like vomit. I put her back into the bed and leaned over Beth and snapped on the bed-light. The baby was wet with vomit and her hair was matted with it and when I began to wipe her, she woke up and whimpered and made a noise back in her throat.

"A drink, sweetheart. Come on, we'll get a drink," I said and picked her up and went into the kitchen. The strong light made her push her head against my neck to hide her eyes. When she heard the water running, she took her head away and blinked her eyes in the light.

I held the glass of water to her lips. She began to strain and gulp the water down, and her hands were stiff away from her body and shaking.

"You poor, thirsty little kid," I said.

The shaking slowed up and stopped as she drank. It was like putting out a fire that was burning inside of her. Finished, she leaned her head against mine. I put the glass down and put out the light. In the hallway, going back to the bedroom, she straightened up and vomited the water.

"Better wake up your mother, kid."

Holding the baby in my arms, I shook Beth. She did not wake up, so I shook her again and she said something and pushed my hand away.

"For Chrissake, get up, Beth," I said, shaking her hard. "I never saw anybody sleep like you can."

"What's the matter?" Her voice was thick with sleep.

"The baby vomited. I gave her some water and she vomited again. I think maybe we better give her an enema."

Beth got slowly out of bed. "Get the bag and bring the big blanket—come to mother, darling."

She took the baby from me and went into the bathroom.

"Let the hot water run, so the room will warm up," I called to her. I heard the water turned on.

I went into the bathroom with the enema-bag and the blanket. Beth was taking the castile soap out of the medicine chest. At the sight of the bag, the baby began to cry.

"Don't cry," Beth said. "Mother won't hurt you."

I spread the blanket on the floor, filled the bag with warm water and dropped the soap into the bag and shook it. Beth put the baby on the blanket; she lay there on her side, crying softly.

"Hold it," I said and gave the bag to Beth. She held it above her head.

Kneeling near the baby, I inserted the tube and she began to cry louder. I held the tube with one hand and held her feet with the other so she could not kick.

"Don't cry, baby," Beth said. "It'll be over soon. Mother doesn't want to hurt you, darling—Buck, don't hold her so tight; you're hurting her. It isn't necessary to hold her so hard."

"She'll kick if I don't."

"You don't have to hold her so tight."

"I'm not hurting her."

"I think that's enough."

"Give her a little more."

"She has a lot now."

"It can't hurt her. Give her a little more."

The baby began to kick, and the water returned out of her.

"Shut it off," I said.

Beth put the bag into the bathtub and picked up the baby. I began to wash my hands.

"My God, just look at that poison coming out of her," Beth said. "I never saw such a stomach on a child. Ever since she was born . . ."

"You stuff her too much," I said.

"I do not. You want her to be as thin as a board."

"You keep on shoving stuff down her throat even when she don't want it."

"She'd never eat if I had to wait for her."

"All right, all right."

I dried my hands on the towel and picked up the blanket.

"Hang it on the window to dry," Beth said. "There's another one in the dresser drawer, the bottom drawer."

When I finished hanging out the blanket, I took the one out of the dresser drawer and spread it on the crib, and Beth brought the baby, changed her nightgown and put her into the crib. The baby looked very white and tired.

Beth got into the bed. I undressed, went into the bed and snapped out the light.

The baby slept and we were not disturbed that night.

XXII

The first thing I did in the morning when I woke up was to raise the blind and look at the baby. She was sleeping very quietly. I pulled the blanket up around her shoulders.

After dressing, I shook Beth. She spoke sleepily.

"Call me up when the baby gets up," I said.

"All right," she said and pulled the covers tighter around her.

I stood looking at her a few moments, then turned around and went out and downstairs.

I walked to the garage. The car was still in the mechanic's hands. I spoke to him and told him that he would have to do a quicker job. He said he was doing his best. A man could not do more than his best. Anyway, fast jobs were bad jobs. If I wanted it done right, I would have to wait. I said I wanted a good job and I wanted it fast and that if he could not do it alone, to get somebody to help him. I wanted it tomorrow, All right, he would have it tomorrow. He looked angry, letting down his eyes and beginning to work while I stood there.

I went out of the garage and walked to the subway and rode downtown.

It was busy in the station-house. Orders were out for activity with results. There was talk of the Commissioner resigning and that this was his farewell cleanup. The rumors made me think of all the years behind me. When Captain Mac asked me who I thought was going in, I said: "How do you know he's going out?"

"Those things get around. You know how those things get around."

"Most of the time, it's a lot of talk."

"Everybody knows it. I guess it's true enough," he said.

"What's the difference who gets it. We got our job to do."

"Can't be worse and it might be better. He's not so hot."

"Did he leave you alone?"

"Sure."

"What else?"

"You getting to like him?"

"No. Only not hating him so much. Not hating anything so much," I said.

"You're getting old and soft. Old and soft."

"Soft—what's soft? I guess it's satisfaction. No more little devils pushing pins into your backside, making you get up and walk around and do and do. Drink and do and fight and crush till you fall down and can't feel the pins anymore. Soft—a wall that keeps the devils out."

"For Chrissake."

"My fault, Mac. I guess I must be getting old."

"Better take a physic, a dose of castor oil."

The telephone bell cut in on the conversation and I answered it.

"It's the same thing, Buck."

"No better."

"No," she said.

"Call the doctor."

"I already did."

"Well, don't get scared."

"O Buck! She just lies there and keeps on crying, 'ma-mama, ma-mama,' and cries for water. I give it to her and she vomits it."

"Don't get scared. Call me up when the doctor goes away."

"I'll call."

I hung up.

"Kid sick?" Mac said.

"Poor kid's been vomiting. I guess it's nothing but an upset stomach."

"She fall down and bang her head? Doctor once told me sometimes banging on the back of the head makes 'em vomit."

"No."

"Must be her stomach."

About twelve o'clock, Beth called me and said that Doctor Shuster had examined the baby.

"It's acidosis."

"What did he tell you to do?"

"He gave me a medicine and told me to give her Kalak water to drink."

"Send the elevator-boy to the drug-store."

"I did. When are you coming home?"

"Soon as I can, Beth."

"Try to get away early. I can't do a thing. I have to be in the bedroom all the time. She cries."

"Don't do a thing then. Be home as soon as I can."

It was late afternoon when she called me again and her voice sounded frightened.

"She fell asleep about eleven and she's been sleeping since."

"She's exhausted," I said. "That's exhaustion."

"It's not natural, Buck. It isn't a natural sleep. I pick her hand up and it just flops back again. That's not sleep."

"Maybe we should call the doctor again?"

"You call him and tell him. Tell him that she doesn't move, just lies there in one position. It's not natural."

"What's the number?"

She gave me the number and said: "Call me right away."

"All right."

I heard her hang up and I juggled the hook up and down until the operator spoke. She connected me with the number. The doctor answered, and I told him.

"What do you think?" I said.

"I think you should have a specialist."

"Who should I call? I don't know any."

"You don't have to call. He wouldn't go if you did. A doctor has to call him. I use Sheffler."

"Can you get him right away?"

"I think so," he said.

"Get him."

"How long will it take you to get home?"

"About forty-five minutes."

"About four o'clock, that is."

"Yes."

"Be there."

I got up from the chair, took my hat and walked to the door and remembered that Beth wanted me to call her. I went back to the telephone and spoke to her.

"Coming right home. The specialist is coming right away."

"Specialist?"

"Don't get scared. I thought maybe we should have a baby specialist."

She said: "All right."

I hung up and went downstairs and outside. A taxicab was passing and I hailed it. Going very quickly, it swerved in to the curb. I gave the driver the address.

"And go like hell," I said. "Don't stop for any lights. I'm Inspector Safiotte."

I got into the cab and slammed the door behind me, and the cab started with a jerk. I leaned forward in the seat.

We went along and something inside kept saying, faster, for Christ sake, faster. Ride, damn, ride. Kick that bastard out of the way—kick that bastard out of the way.

Cars stopped by the traffic lights held us several times. We came near an entrance to the subway. I opened the door of the cab and got out. The driver looked around.

"Getting out here," I said and gave him a bill and walked quickly away.

I went down into the station. A train came along and I got on. I stood up in the car. Jerk, start, stop, and jerk again. Time was a terrible, indefinite thing. Little mother, little baby. If that guy sitting there didn't stop picking his nose, I would kill him. Kill him, kill the goddamn Jew. My toe tapped the floor in irritation. Tap, tap, little mother, little sweetheart. Tap, tap. . . .

The train, at last, drew into the station. I got out and went upstairs. The cool air made me feel better. Walking very fast, I went down the street to the house.

When I opened the door, Beth called, "Who's there?"

"Me, Buck," I said and went down the hallway to the bedroom.

The baby was in her crib. There was a bluish color to her lips and her face was very white. I picked her up and put her on the bed and began to rub her legs. I thought that would stimulate her.

"Daddy's here, darling," Beth said. "Look daddy's here."

The baby opened her eyes, smiled, and closed her eyes again.

"O Buck, that's the first smile she's given today."

"She's all right," I said and rubbed her feet some more. "She's just exhausted."

The door-bell rang.

"That's the doctors, I guess," I said.

Beth went to the door and brought in a small man. He was dirty looking and needed a shave. He said: "Stop that. Don't annoy the child."

I stopped rubbing.

"Didn't Doctor Shuster get here yet?" he asked.

"No," I said.

The specialist came over to the bed and looked down at the baby.

"What seems to be the trouble?"

I told him, beginning at the start of it.

"Now she just lies there like that," Beth said. "It's not a natural sleep, is it, Doctor?"

Doctor Sheffler bent over the baby. He sat her up and lowered her several times and scratched the bottoms of her feet. He felt the top of her head. Then, he took a small flashlight and shined it into the baby's eyes. He stood up and looked at her several minutes; then, took her feet and bent them up several times. While he was doing this, Doctor Shuster came in; he had found the door open.

"Hello, doctor."

"Hello, doctor."

"How are you, doctor?"

"Good. And yourself?"

"Good. You examined the child?"

"Yes. I've examined her. What was your diagnosis? You were here this morning, weren't you?"

"It was a bit too early to judge. It looked to me like acidosis."

"Quite right, quite right. All the symptoms are there. Yet—it might be a cerebral inflammation. She is not very responsive to the light test and her peripherals are not very responsive. The only thing that leads me to believe that it is not an inflammation is the lack of swelling in the open fontanelle—by the way, how is it that the fontanelle is so open at this time? You've been giving her viosterol. Good. She is quite flexive. Have you had her urine examined?"

"I advised it this morning. Mrs. Safiotte hasn't been able to get any."

"Why not, mother?"

"Every time she urinates, she moves her bowels," Beth said.

"You must get it. It is our only means of determining. You must try. Place her on the pan every fifteen minutes, if necessary."

The doctors looked at each other and went into the parlor.

"Buck, go in and hear what they say."

I went into the parlor. They were sitting on the sofa. I sat down in the chair opposite.

"Is it serious?" I said.

"Very serious," Doctor Sheffler said. "Of course, a cerebral inflammation is the more serious of the two. Get some urine and have it examined. That will clinch the diagnosis. Have it examined particularly for iso-butyric acid, diacetic acid, and acetone."

"Here's a place that will be open tonight," Doctor Shuster said and wrote on his pad. "Have them report to me. I'll get in touch with Doctor Sheffler."

"Better write down those names, because I wouldn't remember them," I said.

He wrote them down and handed the paper to me.

"You'd better have a day and night nurse," Sheffler said. "Call up the nurses' registry." He turned to Doctor Shuster, "Write one down for him. The one you use. Tell her to bring a Murphy Drip outfit. The child is to get a drip every three hours. She must have some nourishment. Write this down, doctor—one tablespoonful of bicarbonate of soda and one tablespoonful of glucose to a pint. Also, this prescription."

He dictated a prescription. "And be sure to get diazyme elixir; they sometimes substitute peptenzyme."

I was handed the prescription and the telephone number of the registry.

"Will you call your wife?"

I called her and she came in.

"Mother," Doctor Sheffler said, "your baby will have to get some nourishment."

"She vomits everything. Anyway, now she doesn't want to take anything."

"She must get something. Give her a little malt in some water. No milk—nothing with fat in it. Give her a cracker. A little at a time."

"Have the nurse call me," Doctor Shuster said.

"I'll talk to her. She'll be able to manage it."

"Yes, yes, of course. Also have the nurse give the baby a warm bath and wrap her in a blanket after the bath," the specialist said.

"Even with her fever?" Beth said.

"Yes. Be sure the windows are closed. Be sure to get her urine."

"I'll get it, Doctor."

They got up and took their hats from the table. I asked, how much. The specialist looked embarrassed and Doctor Shuster told me. I paid them. They walked down the hallway and I followed them.

At the door, I said: "Why does she lay there like that? It's not a natural sleep."

"It's the toxicity. That's why I want her to have a warm bath. She can get rid of some of the poison through perspiration. Be sure to get her urine. Good-bye."

"Good-bye," Doctor Shuster said. "Don't forget to tell the nurse to call me."

I closed the door after them and went back to the parlor.

"What did they say, Buck?"

"Nothing much. Stomach trouble. Nothing to get scared about. I'm going out with the prescription. Where's my raincoat? It's raining hard."

She got my coat out of the closet. I put it on.

"Try and get some urine. I'll call the nurse from the drugstore."

"I'll try, Buck," she said and put her hand on my arm and looked at me. "I hope she gets better soon. If she'd only get better. . . ."

"It's only her stomach, Beth. She'll be all right."

She dropped her hand and said: "Go ahead. Make him do it right away."

"He'll make it right away," I said.

I went out on the street. It was dark and raining hard. I pulled my hat down, and the rain ran from it in a little stream.

A distance away, I saw the red and green of the drug-store lights reflected in the wet on the pavements. I came to the drug-store and went in. The clerk was behind the counter. There were no other customers.

"And see that I get diazyme not peptenzyme," I said as I gave him the prescription. "I want it right away."

"About five minutes, sir."

"Is your boss here?"

"No, sir."

"You sure you can make it right?"

He smiled and nodded his head and went into the back room. I went into the telephone-booth and called the registry. They would have a nurse out immediately, they said. One in the morning? A Murphy Drip. All right. Thank you. I hung up the receiver and went out of the booth.

The prescription was not ready and I had to wait. When it was finished, I bought a pound of bicarbonate of soda and a pound of glucose and went out.

When I came into the house and took off my hat and coat and hung them in the kitchen to dry, Beth came in and said: "Will you call them and see if an ounce of urine is enough?"

"Don't think it's enough."

"Call them and see. That's all I could get."

I called the laboratory and was told that an ounce of urine was enough for an analysis.

"Take it right over, Buck."

"What do you think about taking the kid into the parlor? It'll be airier for her and easier for the nurse."

"I was wondering how we would manage."

We went into the bedroom. I put the baby on the bed; she did not move.

"Poor darling," Beth said.

I ran my hand over the baby's legs and bent down and kissed her hand.

"Take her over to the other side of the bed, so she won't get all the dust from the mattress," I said.

Beth moved the baby. I took out the mattress and spring and took the crib apart and set it up in the parlor. Beth put the baby back into it.

I went back to the kitchen and put on my raincoat and went back to the parlor. Beth gave me the bottle and I put it in my pocket.

"I'm going to wait for it, so we'll know."

"Know what, Buck?"

"If it's acidosis."

"What else could it be?"

"It might not be acidosis. Maybe it's not so bad; only a poisoned stomach."

"Well, what's acidosis?"

"Too much fat. I always told you not to feed her butter— well, never mind, you'll know better. I guess I'll take the elevated."

"Isn't the car done yet?"

"No. I bawled him out. I guess I'll take the elevated. That's the nearest."

"Try to get back quick."

XXIII

The laboratory was an apartment in the basement floor of an apartment house. I rang the bell and a woman came to the door and let me in. I wanted to see the chemist, I said. He was busy, she said. Would I leave the specimen and he would call the doctor. No, I said, the doctor told me to wait for the report.

The woman turned around and went into the back of the house. Pretty soon, a man in a white jacket came out. He was entirely bald and his scalp shone in the light and his face was very pink and shiny.

"You wish to see me?" he said. He spoke with a German accent.

"The doctor told me to wait."

"What doctor?"

"Shuster, Louis Shuster."

"On Washington Street?"

"I think so. I think he's on Washington Street. He told me, you should look for iso-butyric acid, diacetic acid, and acetone."

"Yes, yes," he said. "He called me up."

The chemist went to the door in front. "Come in, come in," he said.

I went in after him. There was a long work bench covered with glass apparatus.

"Sit down—there," he said.

I sat down.

"Patient's name? Address? Age? What nonsense—children never have diacetic or iso-butyric acid. Male or female?"

He wrote rapidly and then took some of the urine and put it into a narrow glass tube which he put into a machine like an oven. He threw a switch and a motor started to hum.

I watched him work. Colors: green, red, purple. Drip and drop. Please, iso-butyric and diacetic acid. Drip and drop and jot down on a pad in front of him. He switched off the motor and took the tube out and looked at it. Then, he came over to the table near me and put a glass slide in the microscope on the table and looked through it. When he went to the desk in the corner of the room, I got up.

He wrote, finished and folded the paper and put it into an envelope. I went over to the desk and asked him how much. He told me. I paid him.

"You'll call the doctor?" I said.

"Of course. There's no iso-butyric or diacetic acid. Children never have it. There is a pyolitis."

"What's that?"

"It precedes or follows a contagious disease."

"Between acidosis and a cerebral inflammation, what would you say the urine shows?"

"A cerebral inflammation."

I stood still a moment and looked at him. Then I said "Thank you," and turned around and went out on the street.

It was raining hard. I lifted my face to it and let the water on my face. Rain, storm, sink and drown and die. Sink and drown and die.

Beth met me in the hallway and when she saw my face, she said: "What's the matter, Buck? What's the matter."

"Nothing. I'm wet and cold. It's so damn nasty outside. Is the nurse here?"

"Yes. We gave the baby the warm bath."

"Where's the nurse?"

"She's in the bathroom now. She's been playing with that Murphy Drip for the last half-hour. Go in and see what you can do to hurry her."

"Did she call the doctor?"

"Yes."

I took off my hat and coat and gave them to Beth and went into the bathroom. The nurse was struggling with the rubber hose.

"What's the matter?" I asked.

"Your call was so late. The surgical stores were closed and I couldn't get a Hoffman clamp for the drip. I'm trying to fix this one."

"What kind of a clamp is that—a Hoffman clamp?"

"It clamps on the rubber tube and lets out a drop at a time. I'm trying to fix this one."

"I'll fix it."

I bent the clamp several times, each time it either shut the water off entirely or allowed it to run too freely. Finally, I tied it with a string and pinched it several times and it worked perfectly.

The nurse went into the kitchen with it and I followed her. She looked at me and smiled.

"You don't mind," I said. "I feel better if I do something."

"No, I don't mind," she said and lit a flame under a pan of water that Beth had given her.

Beth sat in a chair and watched us. Several wet sheets were on the floor.

When the water boiled, the nurse put a tablespoonful of glucose and bicarbonate of soda into it and stirred until they dissolved. Then she held the bag and said: "Pour some in. Not all of it. It cools very quick because it drips so slow. If you keep some of it hot, you can keep the rest warm by pouring in a little at a time."

I poured a little into the bag and she went into the parlor.

Beth spoke: "They're so sloppy. Take a look at those sheets. Five of them. There was no necessity for it. They're so sloppy."

"What's the difference?" I said. "Send them to the laundry."

The nurse came in with the outfit still in her hands. "What will we hang this on?" she said.

I went into the parlor with her.

"What about the bridge-lamp? You can put a string through that hole and hang it on."

I got a piece of string and fixed it on the bridge-lamp and put the lamp on the foot-stool near the crib.

"How's that?" I said.

"Fine," she said and rubbed vaseline on the rubber tube.

She inserted the rubber tube. The baby did not move.

"Open the clip. All right. Pinch it a little, it's too fast."

When I pinched the fixed clip, the water slowed up.

I went around to the other side of the crib and knelt down and took the baby's hand in my hands.

"Why don't you two go to bed?" the nurse said.

We were sitting in the parlor. The nurse and I were on the couch and Beth was sitting on the chair.

"Go ahead, Beth," I said. "You're sleepy; I'm not."

"I think I will. I'm tired. Aren't you tired, Buck?"

"No. Going to stay up and help. Go ahead."

"You go too. I can do without help. You're tired too," the nurse said.

"No, I'm staying. Go on, Beth."

She got up and went into the bedroom and there was the sound of her movements as she undressed and then the creak of the bedspring as she got into the bed.

We sat there, the nurse and I. Only the bridge-lamp was burning and it was dim in the room. The baby was a darker shadow in the crib. The ticking of the clock on the piano was loud in the stillness. It was that way for a long while; three hours of it. Then the nurse went into the kitchen and prepared another injection. I held the bag and she poured it in and hung it on the lamp. She inserted the tube and I opened the clip and pinched it and the water, dripped slowly.

"Get me a pan. She's not retaining it. It's coming out. Hurry up—here, the bed-pan's under the crib."

I picked up the porcelain bed-pan and gave it to her. She disconnected the insertion tube and the green filth ran out of it into the pan. She connected it and disconnected it several times.

"She's not retaining at all," she said. "At least, she's getting rid of some of the poison."

"Isn't that what it's for?"

"No. A drip is to feed. When a patient can't retain anything on the stomach, then we feed that way."

"I thought it's an enema."

"No. But it can't hurt her to get rid of some of the poison that way."

Presently, after pouring more water into the bag several times, it was finished. The nurse took the bag into the kitchen and put it into the sink and I heard the glass parts clink against the sink as they struck. She came back and said: "Don't you think you'd better go to bed?"

"I guess I will," I said. "I'm tired. Call me if you need me. Just come in and call me. I don't sleep hard. Will you call me?"

"Yes."

"If it gets cold, there's an electric heater in that closet. Don't be afraid to call me."

I went into the bedroom, undressed, and got into the bed. I could not rest. Thinking, to keep thoughts from creeping in, kept me awake. I heard the nurse moving around and finally, it went further and further away and the last I heard was the clinking of glass against metal. And I dreamed that the baby was grown into a woman with straight legs and rounded breasts.

"Mr. Safiotte, Mr. Safiotte, get up."

I woke up and jumped out of bed. My body was wet with perspiration and the draught through the window chilled me.

"What?" I said. "What?"

We went quickly into the parlor.

"What's the matter?"

"Her pulse and respiration are very low."

"Call the doctor," I said.

"I did. He's at a physician's meeting. They promised to call him."

"Physician's meeting, now?"

"They usually hold them at night."

"What should we do?"

"There's nothing we can do."

"What do you mean, nothing! What the hell do you mean, nothing! Do something! Call another doctor. Here, rub her arms, I'll rub her feet. That'll make her pulse beat."

The nurse looked at me and turned around and said, "All right."

She rubbed the baby's hands and I rubbed her feet. O God, Jesus Christ, have a heart. Give a guy a break! Take it all. I'm only asking for a little thing like this. Why should a little thing like this make any difference to you with the whole world. I'll make it up to you. Little mother, little sweetheart, wake up and look at me. Heart of my heart! O Christ, tearing my heart away . . .

"You'll have to stop, you'll have to stop rubbing, mister."

"Rub, for Chrissake, rub," I said.

"She's gone," she said and turned around and went into the kitchen.

I stood, still holding the baby's foot, then I put it down and got down on my knees and put my forehead against the back of her hand. The nurse came in again.

"You go home now. Come back tomorrow for your pay and the rest, only go home now. I don't want to see you."

"I'll wait for the doctor."

"Go home, now."

She went to the closet and took her coat and hat and put them on.

"Shall I call your wife?"

"No, let her sleep."

"I'm sorry," she said.

"Go home."

"Better put her arms on her breast or you'll have to break them," she said and went down the hallway. I heard the door close.

Little mother. What a dirty, lousy trick. It didn't even get a chance to live. Little mother. O God! Our Father—to hell with that; why, you bloody, murdering—no, no, I didn't mean that. Be good to her like I was, like I would've been. Where she is, be good to her.

I knelt with my head on her hand a long time and the hand was cool now. The dawn came up and the light came into the room and it was chill and grey.

Better put her arms up now. Break those arms. O God, break those arms!

The arms were a little stiff, but they bent when I pushed hard.

I got up. "Better tell your mother, now."

Beth was sleeping, her head pushed high on the pillow, her mouth a little open. I pushed her shoulder and she moved and opened her eyes and looked up at me. I tried to stop myself from swaying back and forth, resting on my heels, then on my toes, but I could not. The color went out of her face when she saw me and her hand went up to her breast and squeezed so hard that I saw the flesh bulge between her fingers.

She said: "What's the matter?" and her voice was hoarse.

"Baby," I said.

She turned around with her face away from me and lay there a few moments and then turned back and got slowly off the bed, the edge of the bed catching her nightgown and sliding it up so that the white straight legs were exposed, and in this time of its death, I saw the moment of its life and saw two white legs tied to the posts of a delivery table and pulling in pain.

I made as though to follow her and she said down in her throat: "Please, Buck," and went into the parlor. I heard the rattle of the metal crib, and then it came. It was so bad that I went in, but when I saw her sitting on the floor, beating the crib with her fist in time with what was hitting her inside, I went to the window. She did not look up when I passed her.

The terrible crying slowed up and died away to a low moaning and she began to talk and cry. She had her baby again and went through all the pain of having it; she watched it grow and then it began to call its mother and to walk and fall and she kissed it where it was hurt; and she felt its arms around her, its soft, wet, sweet-smiling lips on her cheeks; and then, it died—O God, and then, it died.

"That's what we get, Buck."

When she said that, my head went forward and hit the frame of the window. I did not feel any pain.

The crank who played the radio in the morning must have switched on the machine. The music of a jazz orchestra came to us. Jazz and tears and death. That was it: jazz and tears and death.

A newsboy came down the street, shouting, "Paper, extra, paper. Commissioner resigns," his voice getting louder as he came nearer and dying out as he went away, and all that was left was the sound of her low voiced crying mixed with the jazz music.

P. J. WOLFSON
(1903-1979)

Pincus Jacob Wolfson was born in New York City on May 22, 1903, the son of Russian immigrant parents. Though his father was a plumber, Wolfson enrolled in Fordham University and studied to be a pharmacist. In 1926, he married Billie Marmon, and they had three children together. It was while working as a pharmacist in the early 1930s that he began writing Bodies Are Dust. Hollywood took notice, and Carl Laemmle Jr. but him under contract to Universal. Three more novels quickly followed. But Wolfson soon moved into film, writing scripts and producing numerous films, even directing one movie. Wolfson's early career was heavily influenced by Prohibition and coming of age in New York City, but he lived most of his life in Southern California. He died in Calabasas, California, on April 16, 1979.

Bibliography

Bodies Are Dust, Vanguard 1931
    original title, Lion Books 1952
    as *Hell Cop*, Berkley 1960
    original title, Staccato Crime/Stark House, 2021
Summer Hotel, Vanguard 1932
All Women Die, Vanguard 1933
    as *This Woman Is Mine*, Popular Library 1951
    as *Three of a Kind*, Berkley 1959 and 1962
Is My Flesh of Brass?, Vanguard 1934
    as *Pay for Her Passion*, News Stand Library 1949
    as *The Flesh Baron*, Lion Library 1954
    original title, Berkley 1958
How Sharp the Point, Pyramid 1959

Also From Stark House Press:

Black Gat Books is a line of mass market paperbacks introduced in 2015 by Stark House Press. New titles appear every other month, featuring the best in crime fiction reprints. Each book is size to 4.25" x 7", just like they used to be, and priced at $9.99. Collect them all.

Stark House Press

1315 H Street, Eureka, CA 95501 707-498-3135
griffinskye3@sbcglobal.net www.starkhousepress.com
Available from your local bookstore or direct from the publisher

Made in the USA
Monee, IL
31 July 2021

74387940R00118